· The · MARSH ROAD MYSTERIES

CROWNS and CODEBREAKERS

ELEN CALDECOTT

BLOOMSBURY
LONDON NEW DELHI NEW YORK SYDNEY

Bloomsbury Publishing, London, New Delhi, New York and Sydney

First published in Great Britain in July 2015 by Bloomsbury Publishing Plc
50 Bedford Square, London WC1B 3DP

www.bloomsbury.com
www.elencaldecott.com

A CIP catalogue record for this book is available from the British Library

ISBN 978 1 4088 5271 2

MIX
Paper from
responsible sources
FSC® C020471

Typeset by RefineCatch Limited, Bungay, Suffolk
Printed and bound in Great Britain by CPI Group (UK) Ltd, Croydon CR0 4YY

1 3 5 7 9 10 8 6 4 2

About the author

Elen Caldecott graduated with an MA in Writing for Young People from Bath Spa University. Before becoming a writer, she was an archaeologist, a nurse, a theatre usher and a museum security guard. It was while working at the museum that Elen realised there is a way to steal anything if you think about it hard enough. Elen either had to become a master thief, or create some characters to do it for her – and so her debut novel, *How Kirsty Jenkins Stole the Elephant*, was born. It was shortlisted for the Waterstones Children's Prize and was followed by *The Mystery of Wickworth Manor* and *The Great Ice-Cream Heist*. Elen lives in Bristol with her husband, Simon, and their dog.

www.elencaldecott.com

Check out the **Elen Caldecott Children's Author** page on Facebook

Also by Elen Caldecott

CROWNS and CODEBREAKERS

To Emma Mai with love

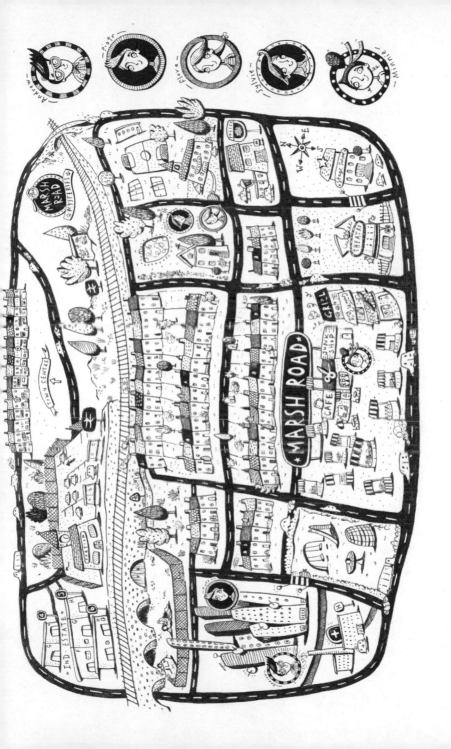

Chapter One

Minnie Adesina was scowling at her bedroom. Specifically, she was scowling at the new bed in her bedroom. The bed that didn't belong. Andrew was sitting on it.

'If the wind changes, your face will stay like that,' he said.

Minnie's scowl deepened.

'If it does,' Andrew added, 'we could rent you out as an extra for horror films. You look like a zombie witch.'

'No, I don't!' Minnie said. 'And it's not true about the wind changing making your face stick … is it?'

Andrew nodded solemnly. 'It happened to a cousin of mine. His face stuck like a Botox disaster. He had to get a job as a miner because he can only go out in the dark.'

Minnie's jaw dropped.

Then Andrew laughed.

Argh! He was just teasing her. Minnie launched herself on to the new bed and pummelled his arm.

'Ow! Get off! Get off! You'll mess up the sheets!'

She stopped. The sheets were crumpled. But there wasn't enough room for her to straighten them properly. She felt cross all over again. Her *old* bed was pushed right up against one wall. The *new* bed, the scowl-worthy bed, was squished in, like a puzzle piece, under the window. There wasn't enough space for two beds. If she wanted to open her curtains, she was going to have to climb over the new one. If she wanted to get clothes out of her wardrobe, well, actually, she couldn't. The new bed stopped the door from opening. She was condemned to wear the same outfit forever and ever.

While Minnie's dad had been assembling the new bed from a flat-pack that made him swear quite a lot, she'd whined, 'Where will I do my homework?' Dad had smirked and said, 'Chance would be a fine thing.' That had been the beginning, middle and end of the discussion.

'You might even like it,' Andrew said. He tried to push her old Hello Kitty duvet flat while he was still sitting on it. It didn't work. The duvet stayed stubbornly rumpled. 'Grans are nice.' Andrew patted the duvet as though it were a tolerant Labrador. 'They give you money and sweets and let you stay up late.' Andrew only saw his gran once or twice a year and he always came away richer.

'I hardly know my gran. I haven't seen her since we visited Nigeria, and that was five years ago. And now she's going to be sleeping ten centimetres away from me.'

'I think it's actually eight centimetres,' Andrew said.

Mum popped her head around the door. It was the only part of her that would fit into the room. 'Andrew, thanks for your help, but you'd better go. They'll be here any minute.'

Andrew gave the duvet one last heavy pat and wiggled sideways out of the room. 'Me and Piotr will be in the cafe,' he said, 'if you need somewhere to hide.' Then he was gone.

Minnie nodded grimly. Her room wasn't hers to hide in any more. She'd *definitely* be seeing Andrew and Piotr later.

They were her best friends. Flora too. She was glad that she had people to moan to about this weird, unwelcome, annoying change. Why did she have to give up all her floor space to Gran? It wasn't fair. Her room was already tiny; now it wasn't even hers.

She scowled up at the ceiling.

Moments later, Minnie heard Dad's key in the lock. Then the sound of bustling from the hallway. Thumps of luggage. Coats coming off. Mum sounding too enthusiastic. A half-mumbled reply.

Then, 'Minnie, come and say hello to Gran.'

Minnie sat up. She thought about checking her reflection in the mirror – Mum would want her to look nice and neat. The mirror was stuck to the inside of the wardrobe door. She pulled it open, but the door banged straight into the new bed and jammed there. She was never going to be able to see her reflection ever again.

She just had to pat down her hair and hoped she looked OK.

As soon as she reached the crowded hall, she knew she didn't.

Mum took one look at Minnie's jeans and T-shirt, and flashed her eyes to heaven. Fashion fail. Apparently jeans were the wrong thing to meet relatives in. Luckily, Dad was more interested in the chaos of luggage he was trying to fit through the door.

And Gran?

Gran just looked over-the-moon-and-back-again happy. Her face was wrinkled into a map of smiles. She held her arms open and pulled Minnie into a hug. 'Ah, my granddaughter! You are grown, oh. You will be tall like your late grandpa.' All the time that Gran spoke, Minnie was smothered into the bright fabric of her dress, her eyes closed to stop Gran's electric blue headwrap poking into them. Minnie felt tall and skinny mashed into this small, round lady who smelled of spice and heat and flowery perfume.

Minnie felt suddenly very shy. Luckily, Gran did enough talking for the both of them. 'Your cousins send their love. Your aunties too. I have brought pictures. Your second cousin Temi has graduated top of his year. His brother is cross, but two rams can't drink from the same bowl, I always say. Your auntie's cousin, Yekemi, was married. Shame you could not come to the wedding.' Gran spoke in a broad Lagos accent, like Dad's, with 'a's like 'ah's. Minnie was finally released from the hug. She stood stock-still, trying to take the whirlwind of family news in.

Mum gave her a small smile. Apparently the jeans were forgiven.

'Would you like some tea?' Mum said quickly as Gran paused for breath. 'You must be tired after the flight.'

Gran gave a long sigh. 'It's true. My throat is drier than the Sahara! I can barely speak a word, oh. I could not sleep on the aeroplane. I was too excited. To be coming to England to see my son and his wonderful family. And his wonderful home. Also, the engine was very loud. I had to shout to be heard. Tea. Yes.'

Mum took Gran's coat and hung it on one of the hooks beside the door. 'Well, Mama, come and sit down in the living room,' she said.

'Oh, but I have a treat for you. I have brought hibiscus tea from Lagos. Grown right in the heart of Nigeria.'

Hibiscus tea? Wasn't that a flower? Minnie glanced, alarmed, at Mum.

'Don't you want to try English tea?' Mum said. 'It's the national drink, you know.'

Gran laughed, a full, throaty noise that seemed to fill up the hallway and the rooms beyond. 'I've tried English tea before. Nasty stuff. We'll have hibiscus today.'

'All right,' Mum said, in a funny, tight voice. 'We'll have that. Whatever you like.'

'I'll take your luggage to your room, Mama,' Dad said. 'You're in with Minnie.'

Gran had three cases, two big red ones and one small black one, as well as a huge handbag and three plastic carrier bags. Dad managed to grab the big cases, but the third was too much.

'Help your dad,' Mum said to Minnie.

'And get my tea for me,' Gran added. 'It's in the black case.'

Minnie picked up the black case and followed Dad into the bedroom. He put the two big cases on to the scowl-worthy new bed, Gran's bed – there was nowhere else for them. 'It'll be cosy,' Dad said hopefully. Then he left in a hurry.

Minnie put the black case on her own bed.

Tea. She needed to find Gran's tea. Who drank flower tea? How weird was that?

The black case had a zip that ran around the edge and a clasp that went over that. It looked a bit battered and dusty from the flight. Gran would probably rub it down with a spitty hankie when she noticed.

Minnie opened it. And was confused.

She had been expecting Lagos tea, Nigerian snacks, a few big, print dresses or over-sized knickers.

But she wasn't looking at anything like that.

Inside the case were some very small shorts, an orange T-shirt – child sized with a crocodile logo – a pair of small boys' trainers and a piece of paper. There was also a battered-looking teddy bear with mangy fur and an eye missing.

Why was Gran carrying around boys' clothes? It didn't make sense.

Minnie closed the lid of the suitcase. And wondered. It was a perfectly ordinary plain black suitcase. There must be thousands of cases just like it. There were probably at least ten cases just like it on Gran's flight alone. All of them going around the airport carousel at the same time.

Plenty of black cases that an excited, tired Gran could have reached for instead of her own.

She opened the lid again. It was still full of boys' clothes.

Gran was not going to like this, not one bit.

Chapter Two

Minnie was going to have to tell Gran that her hibiscus tea, and everything else that had been in the black case, was missing. She had picked up the wrong case at the airport.

Perhaps it would be better coming from Dad? Or Mum? They would be much better at that sort of thing. Gran was going to be so upset.

Minnie was just about to yell and ask Dad to come back, when something caught her eye – and made her pause.

Inside the case, just next to the chewed-too-often teddy, was what she'd thought was a piece of paper. But, she realised, it was a postcard. It should have been a cheery picture. Once, the postcard had shown five boys sitting in bright sunshine on a bleached wooden jetty above diamond and sapphire blue water. Once.

Now, though …

Minnie reached down to pick it up. She realised her hand was shaking. The postcard was horrible now. The boys' eyes had been neatly snipped from the image. Their mouths were open and smiling, probably calling out to the photographer like street-hawkers. But their eyes were just empty squares with sharp edges; she could see the pale brown pads of her own fingertips peeking through.

Who would cut boys' eyes from a picture? And why?

She'd heard stories from her second cousins and the other children in Lagos about victims being kidnapped, being used for juju – dark magic. Children disappearing underground and never being seen again. She hadn't believed the stories. Of course she hadn't.

But this postcard looked nasty. Like those stories had been.

She flipped it over.

There was a scrawled message on the back: *Post in two days.* Printed in tiny letters was a description of the scene: *Boys pose at Bar Beach, Lagos, Nigeria.*

She looked at the front again. The missing eyes made her think of spirit masks and monsters, and her cousins and cousins' cousins laughing because the British girl was scared to switch off the light at night.

She should tell Dad.

She should tell Andrew! He would love this. A piece of real juju!

There was a camera on her phone. It would be wrong to take the postcard to show Andrew: it didn't belong to her, after all. And it was creepy. But a photo was the next best thing. She snapped the front and back of the card. How long did she have to stay indoors, she wondered, before she could go and show the others?

Probably longer than she wanted.

She put the card back on the orange T-shirt and closed the lid.

Time to break the news about the missing tea to Gran. She walked slowly into the living room.

Gran was sitting in the armchair that was usually Mum's. Mum and Dad sat across from her on the sofa. They all looked like they were posing for a portrait, with their best smiles and their awkward angles. Even the ragged terracotta walls that Mum had been so proud of doing herself looked like the pull-down backdrop of school photos.

Everyone looked her way.

'Gran,' she said, 'I'm sorry, but I don't think the black case you've got is your black case.'

Gran's set smile wobbled. 'What do you mean to say?'

'I think … well … you'd best go and see. But there won't be any hibiscus tea today.'

Gran got to her feet with a sigh and left the room. Dad followed behind. Then Mum raised her hands and said, 'What now?' before going with them.

Minnie sat on the sofa and waited.

It wasn't long before she heard a shriek. Yup, it definitely wasn't Gran's case.

Gran came back first, her hands flapping like bats in front of her face. Mum was next, promising sweet tea for the shock, even though it would have to be the non-Lagos kind. Dad came last, holding his phone, promising to find the number of the airline, the airport, the pilot of the plane, the owner of the company, anyone at all who might be able to get Gran's case back for her.

Minnie wondered if anyone would notice if she slipped out and went to find Andrew, Piotr and Flora?

'Minnie,' Mum said, apparently reading her mind, 'stay with Gran. Calm her down.'

Mum left the room to fetch sugar with added tea. Dad left to make some calls.

Minnie was left with Gran.

Gran sat down heavily. Her hands, with fingers so round it wasn't clear that they could bend, came together in a clasped prayer. 'It's a sign,' she said sadly. 'It's a true sign.'

'What is?'

'The tea leaves. It's a bad omen. Tea leaves know the future. Some people can read their whole lives in the bottom of a cup. And these leaves, oh! They didn't survive the journey. What does that say, eh?'

Minnie was pretty certain that the tea leaves weren't saying anything at all – except that maybe Gran needed to be more careful at airports. But she knew this wasn't the time to say anything.

Gran's hands were still clasped tight in her lap, the lines on her face set, like a compass needle, to Worry.

'They'll get it back, I'm sure,' Minnie said.

'No.' Gran shook her head. 'It has gone. For good. I can feel it.'

Maybe this was the reason why Gran had come to stay, because she was scared of random things? Minnie had overheard conversations between Mum and Dad for months now: Dad worrying about his mum, so far away; Mum not sure that being in a little flat above a shop was better for Gran than being in the city she'd always known, with friends and neighbours. But Dad was Gran's eldest child. 'A river that forgets its source dries up,' he'd said to Mum. Then, when poetry hadn't worked, 'She'll be no trouble. We'll hardly even notice she's here.'

Despite all of Dad's efforts, no one knew whether Gran was going to stay forever or not. They would have to see. But if she was taking advice from tea, Minnie reckoned, then Gran probably did need to stay.

'I had dreams that this would happen,' Gran said, interrupting Minnie's thoughts.

'What? You dreamed you'd pick up the wrong case?'

Gran tutted against her teeth. 'I dreamed that I would forget my home, and it would forget me.'

That didn't sound a lot like losing a suitcase. Still, Minnie decided it was better not to argue. But Gran must have been able to read her face, because she said, 'You think I am foolish? I am not. You should listen to dreams. Just as you should listen to your stomach growl when you're hungry. Dreams are your spirit growling. The king of Ife is very sensitive to dreams. He once stopped an archaeological dig because his ancestors were disturbing his sleep. They stomped through his dreams every night, clattering pans and banging drums. The king got no rest for weeks.'

'Who's the king of Ife?' Minnie asked.

Gran frowned. 'Your great-grandparents were from Ife, my mother and father. It's where I grew up. It's an ancient city, some say the oldest in Nigeria. Hasn't your father told you that?'

Minnie shook her head. Dad was more likely to tell her the football scores or his opinion on the latest Disney film than he was to tell her about dreams and kings and great-grandparents. Or tea. She was beginning to think that having Gran around might be more interesting than she'd bargained for.

Mum came in then, so Minnie didn't have to reply. Which was good, as she could think of absolutely nothing to say. Mum handed a steaming mug of tea to Gran.

Gran took it with a sigh. 'Thank you, Taiwo,' she said. 'Minnie was just telling me that she doesn't listen to dreams.'

Mum's smile was the sort of smile she used when she realised she'd accidentally cut someone's hair too short. 'I'll just go and see how Dad's getting on with the airline,' she said.

Dad was not getting on well.

Minnie could hear him and Mum whispering in the hallway. It sounded a lot like, 'You tell her,' 'No, you tell her,' but Minnie couldn't be sure.

Gran sipped her tea slowly.

Finally Dad came in. 'I'm sorry, Mama,' he said, 'but the airline don't know where your bag is. It isn't at the airport. Maybe one of the other passengers took it. The one whose bag you have perhaps?'

Gran tilted her head. Her blue headwrap swayed impressively. 'Then they must call the passenger.'

'They have. The number on their record doesn't connect though. I'm sorry, but they said we'll have to wait for the passenger to get in touch.'

'*Tsk*. My luggage was labelled properly, with my name and the address I'm staying at. Why could the other passenger not have done the same with their case, hmm? Then we could go to them, and we would not have to sit around waiting for them to call the airline. I bet it was the boy I saw travelling on his own. He was a tiny little thing, though he ate the whole flight. The air stewards made sure he had his own body weight in free peanuts. He was too young to fly alone, I thought. And see! Too young to know about labelling luggage properly.'

'I'm sure his family will get in touch with the airline once they realise the mistake,' Mum said.

Gran looked disgusted. 'Do you really think someone

16

will return Lagos's finest hibiscus tea for some cheap boys' clothes and a torn postcard?'

Torn? Gran made it sound like a forgotten bit of rubbish. Was that all it was? Minnie opened her mouth to speak. Then closed it again. She'd felt something holding that postcard, a sense of menace. Whatever Gran thought, Minnie knew there was something badly wrong with that juju card.

And she was certain that whoever owned it would want it back.

Chapter Three

The phone didn't ring for the rest of the evening. Mum and Dad did their best to make Gran forget her missing luggage. Mum had cooked jollof rice to celebrate Gran's arrival. Gran picked at it, pushing the grains around with her fork.

'Is it all right?' Mum asked.

'Delicious,' Gran said, without taking a mouthful. 'Really lovely. But I can't help thinking about my tea.'

'Don't worry,' Dad said. 'There's an Indian shop on the high street. They might have hibiscus tea.'

'Why would an Indian shop have Nigerian tea?' Gran asked, baffled.

Dad shrugged. 'It's the way of it.'

Gran nodded. 'I see. I thought I was ready to come here, oh. I thought I was prepared. But now, I do not know. Men make plans, but God acts.'

Gran sounded so low that Minnie reached out and rubbed her shoulder. She wanted to say, 'It's only tea.' But she was beginning to see that, for Gran, it wasn't only tea. It was a new life, a new country, new rules. If an old woman didn't know where to buy her favourite tea, that woman might well feel lost.

The kitchen table, which had always been fine for three of them, felt overcrowded today. Everyone touching elbows and reaching for someone else's drink.

'You'll feel better after a good night's sleep,' Mum said.

Gran smiled gratefully.

They all went to bed early. The grown-ups seemed relieved the day was over.

Minnie let Gran get ready for bed in their room. Minnie went to the bathroom and brushed her teeth slowly. She got changed into her pyjamas. Was it going to be like this forever? Stepping out of jeans while trying not to fall and crack her head on the sink? Gran was weird and interesting, but she would be three hundred times better if she had her own room. Minnie sighed and bundled up her clothes in her arms.

She edged her way into her room. There was nowhere to put her bundle, so she left it beside the door. Gran was already under the Hello Kitty duvet, reading a small black book. She was wearing a nightdress that came right up under her chin. Without her headwrap, Gran's hair was short and grey. Minnie noticed a thick black wig on a plastic head on the window sill. Gran noticed her looking and laughed. 'I get to change my hair every day if I like!'

'Mum's got some pink wigs in the salon. You could have one of those.'

'Or a Mohican, like a London punk!' Gran laughed. 'I think I would like that. Or maybe a head of hair beaded red and orange and bronze, like the crown of a king!'

Minnie pulled back her duvet and settled against the crisp white pillowcase. 'Are crowns made of beads?' she asked. 'I thought they were gold.'

'Not always. The queen here might have gold and jewels, but Yoruba kings have mighty headdresses fashioned from intricate beadwork. They are beautiful, but a little scary too. They have eyes that watch you, the gaze of the ancestors.'

'The kings of Ife?'

'Exactly,' Gran said firmly. She lifted her book again.

'Good book?' Minnie asked.

'*The* good book,' Gran corrected. 'The New Testament.'

Oh.

'It tells us to be strong when we face the world,' Gran said. 'Though I also like to remember the old story that we were made from dirt in a snail's shell, so I don't feel too bad if I don't manage to be brave all the time.'

Minnie snuggled under her own duvet. The sound of Gran turning the thin pages was like a gentle whisper, lulling her to sleep.

Breakfast on Sunday morning was weirdly, horribly early. Minnie usually liked to lounge about in her pyjamas, watching cartoons for a bit, even though she was too old for that sort of thing really. But, at half past eight, cereal was on the table. When Minnie asked why, Mum hissed that they were going to church. She also hissed that if Minnie could manage not to mention to Gran that this wasn't a regular event, then Mum would be very grateful.

'Grateful enough to let me have my ears pierced?' Minnie asked hopefully.

'No. Go and get ready. Wear a dress.'

'Can Andrew and Piotr come?'

Mum sighed. 'Fine. Ask them. But even if they say no, you're coming anyway.'

Thankfully, Piotr and Andrew did want to come along. They agreed to be at the salon below the flat in thirty minutes, wearing their best clothes.

Back in her room, Minnie clawed a hand into her wardrobe and, like a bear hunting salmon, fished out a slippery pink affair. She glared at the satin dress with its lace collar and puffy sleeves, and sighed.

She pulled off her pyjamas and jammed her arms into the sleeves. It was like being gripped by a frilly vice. 'It doesn't fit!' she shouted.

There was no reply from Mum in the kitchen.

'I'm stuck!' She wriggled and just managed to jam her head in the neck. She was pinned, forced into submission by pink froth. Her arms were stuck right up as though she were a bystander at a bank robbery.

'I'm stuck!' she yelled again.

'Minnie!' Mum's voice was closer now, in the room.

Minnie felt Mum's hands on the material, tugging up, then down, then up again.

'You might have to cut me out,' Minnie said hopefully.

'No way. There are at least two good wears in this dress still. Breathe in.'

Minnie took a deep lungful of air and tried to pretend

22

she didn't have ribs. Mum yanked and tugged and hoicked, and finally the dress was on.

'I won't be able to sit down in church, you know,' Minnie said.

'Then you'll just have to lean against the pew,' Mum said. 'Let's go.'

Gran had obviously been ready for ages. This time with a hat on her head instead of a wrap. She stood impatiently at the door, while everyone else got shoes and coats and bags.

Piotr and Andrew were already outside the salon, Andrew in what looked a lot like his school uniform; Piotr had managed to find a dark shirt. They both stared at her dress in horror, as though she was wearing slices of meat instead of satin.

'Yes, all right,' she said. 'I can wear a dress sometimes.'

They weren't the only ones to stare.

There was a bench in the street outside and some older boys were sitting on it. Minnie felt herself blush as she walked past them and heard them comment. She was basically Church Barbie. It was a nightmare.

She kept her head down all the way to St Michael's, barely glancing at the theatre or shops as they walked.

As far as she was concerned, the ground outside Ahmed's Cleaners could happily open up and swallow her.

They all trooped into the church and found a row of seats together. The hall was warm, cosy and very modern, with a PA system to make the sermon easier to hear. After they sang a few hymns and listened to the pastor, Gran's wide-as-anything grin was back.

Andrew sang the loudest of anyone there. Piotr mumbled the words so softly that barely a murmur came out. Minnie just tried to stay in tune. Once the service was done, Dad treated everyone to a roast dinner in a family pub. Minnie got mint sauce on her dress accidentally-on-purpose.

Gran led the way back to the flat in a much brighter mood. Minnie swung her arms as much as she could against the tight lace, and raised her face up to the sun. The world might have been made from the dirt in a snail's shell, but some days, she felt, it was very nice dirt.

The feeling didn't last.

Something was wrong inside the salon. She could sense it as soon as they stepped inside.

It was too cold. A breeze was blowing through.

Mum and Dad paused. Gran looked confused. Where was the breeze coming from?

'Stay here,' Dad said.

Minnie, Piotr and Andrew waited.

He went to the back of the salon, then reappeared. 'The back door is wide open,' he said to Mum. 'The lock's been forced.'

Mum looked around. Burglars? What had they taken?

The salon looked pristine. Nothing had been touched.

She ran upstairs. Her heels clattered on the tiles. Minnie and the others followed slowly. The door to the flat had been forced open too, the wood around the lock splintered like firewood.

Mum dashed from the living room, to her bedroom, to the kitchen. 'Nothing's missing,' she said. 'Why would someone break in and take nothing?'

Minnie's skin prickled. She remembered the strange postcard in the wrong case, the missing eyes, the juju. She went into her bedroom.

When they'd left for church that morning, the small black case had been propped against the wardrobe. It was gone.

'They were in my room,' she said softly.

Mum was at her side, then Gran, then Dad. It felt squished, hard to breathe.

Gran sat down heavily on her bed. 'While we were at

church,' she whispered. 'While we were at *church*.' She held her hand to her chest.

Dad sidestepped the bed and sat down beside Gran. 'It's OK, Mama,' he said. 'It's OK.'

'How is this OK? Strangers in our house! Bad people. In our room.' She rolled her eyes to heaven. 'Who would do such a thing? And why would they not just ask for their case? I would have returned it. I am not a criminal!'

All very good questions.

Minnie caught Piotr's eye and flicked her head towards the hallway. He and Andrew followed her out.

They could still hear Dad's soft whispering, Mum's soothing and Gran's rock-solid unshakable belief that they would be murdered in their beds next.

'Is nothing else gone?' Piotr asked. 'No jewellery, or money, or computers?'

Minnie whisked through the rooms, but Mum was right – there wasn't a drawer open, a cupboard ransacked, a single knick-knack out of place. The black case was the only thing missing.

'What's the big deal about the black case?' Andrew said.

Minnie explained quickly about the mix-up on the carousel.

'So it wasn't even your gran's case?' Andrew sounded confused.

Dad came out of the bedroom. He looked at the three of them standing in the hallway. 'You look like hatstands,' he said. 'Why don't you go and watch some TV or something? I'm going to call the police to report the break-in.'

Minnie led the way into the living room. She felt dazed. The terracotta walls, the green sofa, the ordinary everyday things looked like a film set, fake and flimsy.

'Are you OK?' Piotr asked.

She shrugged. *Someone* had broken in, walked around, searched their flat. Not a random burglary either, but someone looking for a particular item. Even the air in the flat felt changed. Dirty.

What was so important that someone felt it was all right to break in?

The juju postcard? The boy's things?

She had to know.

The flat wouldn't feel like home again until she knew. 'Piotr, Andrew, I'm changing out of this stupid dress, then I'm calling Flora and we're getting out of here.'

Chapter Four

The cafe where they usually met was closed on Sundays, so Minnie sat in the window seat of the salon, back in her jeans and T-shirt, watching out for Flora. Andrew sat on one of the salon chairs while Piotr pumped it up as high as it would go. Andrew's legs dangled like fishing lines.

'Here she is,' Minnie said finally. 'Oh. Sylvie's with her.' She said it as though Flora had brought a dripping rubbish bag with her.

'Sylvie's not so bad,' Andrew said. 'You just need to ignore most of what she says.' He picked up three huge hair clips with crocodile teeth and arranged them in a Mohawk on his head. He added two more to the wings of his glasses.

Minnie unlocked the front door and let the twins in.

'Are you all right? Are your family OK?' Flora asked.

'Have you got any biscuits?' Sylvie asked. 'My blood sugar's a bit low.'

Minnie nodded yes to both questions. 'Biscuits. Upstairs,' she said. Minnie gestured for Sylvie to follow. She wasn't about to bring the biscuits down; she was not Sylvie's servant. Sylvie paused to look at the broken back door, but didn't say anything.

The flat was quieter now. There was no sign of Mum. Dad was on the phone. He nodded at Sylvie as they walked past.

Gran was sitting at the kitchen table, a china cup and saucer holding tea the colour of caramel in front of her.

Dad's voice drifted from the hallway. 'I know it wasn't ours. I didn't say it was.'

'Gran, this is Sylvie. Sylvie, Gran.'

Sylvie held out her hand. 'It's a pleasure to meet you, Mrs Adesina,' she said sweetly. 'I'm so sorry to hear about your trouble.'

'You can call me Auntie,' Gran said.

'Thank you, Auntie.'

Minnie's eyes rolled so high she could see her own eyebrows.

'A break-in while we were at church,' Gran said.

'Disgraceful,' Sylvie nodded.

'Disgraceful, yes.'

'Are you all right though, Auntie?' Sylvie asked.

Gran rested her fingertips on either side of her cup, as though to warm them. 'This place is more dangerous than Lagos. This is not what I had expected. But the tea knew.'

'The tea?' Sylvie sounded confused.

'Here –' Minnie said quickly, before Gran could explain. 'Hobnob.'

'Thank you, Minnie,' Sylvie said graciously. 'Auntie, you shouldn't let the break-in worry you. It's very, very unusual. Mostly just nice things happen here. Like the market. That's right on your doorstep. You'll like that.'

'Is it the sort of market,' Gran said, 'where you can spend a whole morning choosing the best vegetables for a pepper soup? Could you argue over the price of cardamom with a man whose family have been spice traders for generations? Can you buy yards of fabric decorated in all the colours of the rainbow and use it to make the finest outfit for everyone to see on Sunday? Is it that kind of market?'

Sylvie smiled. 'That kind of market sounds wonderful,' she said. 'It isn't quite like that.'

'You can argue with the fruit and veg trader if you like,' Minnie said. 'He won't mind.'

Gran shook her head sadly. The kitchen chair creaked as her weight shifted. 'The crime rate in Lagos is bad. "Come live with us," your daddy said. "You'll be safe with us." But look! Rain falls on everyone. As bad here as at home.'

Gran reached for the biscuits and dunked one in her tea. 'And now I am eating between meals too. I am being driven to it.' She sucked the Hobnob. 'But you girls shouldn't. You still have good teeth.'

'It's for me,' Sylvie said sadly. 'I have diabetes, so need to be careful.'

Gran made a sympathetic noise. 'You poor thing. How do you manage?'

Sylvie opened her mouth to speak, but Minnie interrupted. 'She manages just fine,' she said firmly. 'Come on, let's get back.'

'You come and visit anytime,' Gran said to Sylvie. 'You seem like a lovely girl. A good friend for my lovely granddaughter.'

It was all Minnie could do not to shove Sylvie out using the Hobnobs as a cattle prod.

Downstairs, the others were discussing the break-in.

Andrew had taken the clips off his head, presumably to try to look like a serious investigator. That or they were hurting.

Flora watched Minnie and Sylvie walk into the room, her eyes wide with curiosity. 'Do you know what was in the suitcase? Do you think the person who owned it broke in to get it back?'

Minnie pointed the open end of the biscuit packet at Flora. 'I was thinking something like that,' she agreed. The biscuits were passed around and Minnie settled on to the window seat, next to the collection of inspiration magazines that Mum loved.

Flora always carried a backpack covered in badges and key rings. She opened it now and pulled out a new notebook. 'I came prepared,' she said.

Piotr nodded in approval. 'Minnie, why don't you tell us what was in the case? As much as you can remember.'

'Why?' Sylvie said suddenly. 'I mean, your dad is talking to the police right now. This isn't like last time. We're not talking about a Hollywood actress's stolen diamonds here. This is just –'

'What?' Minnie snapped. 'It's just my gran feeling frightened of the place she's come to live? My gran scared of going to sleep in case the burglar comes back? That

32

isn't important enough for you? And I haven't even told you about the little boy!'

Sylvie's lips pressed tight until they were just a sliver of pale skin.

'I don't think that's what Sylvie meant,' Flora said carefully. 'I think she was just saying the police might be better at solving this one than us.'

'Well, they might,' Minnie said after a second's pause to glare at Sylvie. 'But that doesn't mean I can sit by and do nothing while Gran waits for them.'

Andrew grinned. He seemed not to notice tension. 'It will be fun to be investigating again. I think we should.'

Minnie looked at Piotr. He was the unofficial leader of the gang. He sat quietly for a moment, thinking. Then he said, 'I think we should investigate. If the police find the burglar first, then at least the burglar has been found. And if the police don't find him, or her, then we might.'

Minnie felt a weight lift that she hadn't known was there. Her friends would help her make things right for Gran.

'So,' Flora said, lifting her notebook and pen. 'What was in the suitcase?'

Minnie remembered the dusty lid, the battered edges, a case that had travelled all the way from Lagos, specked with grains of the Sahara carried on harmattan winds. She lifted the lid again in her mind. 'An orange T-shirt, a pair of shorts. Trainers. All little boy sized. A teddy bear, all battered and worn like someone had loved it but not washed it very often. And something else, something weird.'

'Weapons? Drugs?' Andrew asked eagerly.

Minnie pulled out her phone and tapped the screen until she found the photo she was looking for. 'No,' she said, turning it around to show them. 'This.'

The others looked.

'Yuck,' Sylvie said. 'Who'd cut the eyes out of boys?'

'It's not their real eyes,' Andrew said. 'It's just their cardboard ones. Probably.'

'You really think your flat was burgled for this?' Sylvie asked. 'Why?'

Minnie felt her face redden. 'I wondered … I wondered whether it might be a, well, a spell or something.'

Even as she said it, she wished she hadn't.

'A spell?' Piotr asked.

'Well, yeah. I met some kids in Lagos last time I was there. They said that children get taken in the night. They lose eyes, fingers, toes to use in juju magic. They're found in the morning, walking blind, beside dusty roads. Gran

34

said she saw a boy alone on the flight. He ate a ton of peanuts. If these clothes are his, and he's being used for juju magic, then he's in real trouble.'

There was silence.

'Whoever broke in,' Flora said finally, 'they had to smash the locks to do it. I don't think much of their magic.'

Minnie flashed Flora a grateful look. At least she hadn't laughed.

'Send me the photo,' Flora said. 'And measure your hand. I can work out how big the postcard was and print off a copy, with a bit of help from Photoshop.'

'What else? Can we find out who the case belongs to?' Piotr asked.

'The airline wouldn't tell Dad yesterday. Data protection. And their phone number didn't work anyway.'

Flora looked thoughtful. 'We need to know who's been near your flat while you were all at church. Any callers? Or deliveries? Or anyone just hanging around?'

Oh.

Minnie knew where to begin. 'We need to get our investigating hats on,' she said.

'Deerstalkers?' Andrew said. 'Cool.'

* * *

The boys who had laughed at Minnie's dress earlier were still there, slouching on the bench. Minnie led the way out of the salon and over to them.

'S'up,' one of the boys said.

He was wearing baggy basketball clothes, as if he'd bought them to grow into. Though he obviously thought he looked cool. He lolled back, loose limbed, against the wooden slats.

'Michael,' Minnie said.

The other boys sniggered.

'It's Lowdog,' Michael said. 'I'm called Lowdog now, yeah?'

Minnie sighed. Michael had been one of the best-behaved boys in Year Six when she'd been in Year Three. All the teachers had loved him. Times had changed.

'Fine. Lowdog. Whatever. Listen, you've been here all day, haven't you?'

Lowdog nodded.

'Well, I wondered, did you see anyone go down the side alley?' She pointed to the narrow gap that ran down beside the cafe. It led to the backyards of the cafe, the salon and the junk shop. It was the only way to get to Minnie's back door.

Lowdog pushed his cap up on his forehead. He tried

to look bored, but couldn't quite manage it. 'Why? Is something going down?'

'Yes.' Andrew stepped forward. 'A burglary went down. Did you see anyone?'

Lowdog thought for a moment. His two friends watched him carefully.

'It's not cool to grass,' he said. 'But then, it's not cool to steal from my hood either.'

'It's not grassing to tell us,' Minnie said.

'Yeah, you're not the Feds,' Lowdog agreed.

Minnie heard Sylvie smother a laugh. She glared at her. Michael-Lowdog might be a bit ridiculous, but he had crucial information; they couldn't afford to annoy him.

He cleared his throat. 'I saw a window cleaner. He had one of those big water-jet backpacks. I thought I'd like a go on that. He did the front of the cafe, then went down the alley to do the back.'

'There was a dry cleaning delivery guy too,' one of the other boys said. 'Remember we said it looked like he was carrying a ghost, cos of that big plastic bag he was waving around?'

Piotr looked interested. 'Was he delivering clean clothes?'

The boy shrugged. 'He went down the alley. But he came back out still carrying the white sack. Maybe he was lost.'

'Did the sack look empty or full when he came out?'

'It looked the same as when he went in, I reckon.'

'Did it have the company name written on it?'

The boy shook his head. 'Nah. It was plain white. But there was something on his cap. It was sick. Better than Lowdog's.'

'Hey!'

'Chill, bro, you know it was. It had an ace of spades on it – well sick.'

Minnie had to shove her hands into her pockets to stop herself from jumping. Two suspects already!

'Was that everyone? No market traders, or shop deliveries, or anything?' Piotr asked.

'That's it, man,' Lowdog said.

'No, wait, there was some weird guy,' the third boy said. 'He took a whole load of photos of the graffiti in the alley, remember? He had that big, old skool camera.'

'What did he look like?' Piotr asked.

'Old white guy, grey hair. Suit. Bow tie. I can show you.' Lowdog pulled out his phone. 'My boy Gnasher here was doing some body popping. He does great robot arms.'

Gnasher looked proud of the praise.

'So I filmed it, yeah?' Lowdog tapped his camera screen. 'The old guy was in the background. It was a bit annoying really. He brings down the cool factor by about eighty per cent.'

Lowdog showed Piotr the screen and the others crowded around. In the background of Gnasher's electrified octopus impression was a tall, thin man with a chunky camera slung around his neck. He was examining the brickwork closely.

'So was *that* everyone?' Minnie asked.

Lowdog nodded and put his phone away. 'I reckon.'

'Thanks,' Piotr said.

'Thanks, *Michael*,' Sylvie said.

The two boys either side of Lowdog sniggered again.

Chapter Five

Minnie stormed back to the salon, with Piotr trotting to keep up. 'What's wrong?' he asked. 'We've got suspects! This is good news.'

'Sylvie!' Minnie said. 'She's not taking this investigation seriously!'

Behind them, Sylvie walked between Flora and Andrew, smiling at nothing.

'Ignore her,' Piotr said. 'She doesn't mean anything by it. It's just how she is.'

'Don't take her side!'

'There aren't any sides,' Piotr said. 'We're in this together.'

It didn't feel like they were in it together. It would be different if it were Sylvie's gran who was scared. Then it would be taken seriously. But Minnie's gran? Sylvie thought it was OK to muck about. Well, it wasn't.

Minnie turned her key and pushed the salon door

open a bit too heavily. It thumped against the wall. Inside, she threw herself into the window seat and stared at Marsh Road as the others trooped in.

It was Piotr who took charge. 'We'll start looking for our suspects and interviewing them first thing tomorrow, when everything's open. There are quite a few dry cleaners in town. Minnie and I can visit them, see if any do Sunday deliveries maybe.'

'I want to find the photographer,' Andrew said.

'How will you do that without knowing his name?' Flora asked.

'I'm not sure,' Andrew replied. 'But I've got a feeling I've seen him somewhere before. I'll work it out. Especially if you help me.'

Flora nodded, her cheeks turning pink. She was obviously pleased to be asked.

'But that leaves me on my own looking for the window cleaner!' Sylvie said in outrage. 'I don't want to be by myself. I want to look for the photographer!'

Did Sylvie think she was too good for a window cleaner? Minnie felt a stab of something like spite. She put on her broadest, sweetest smile. 'What a shame Andrew and Flora have already bagsied him. So you *are* on your own, whether you like it or not.'

Sylvie folded her arms across her chest. Her eyes were angry slits in her face. 'You can't tell me what to do. I don't even know if I believe the peanut boy needs our help. He might just be on holiday. You're the only one who believes in juju magic, or whatever it's called.'

'Sylvie!' Piotr warned.

'It's true!' she insisted. 'They're stories *she* heard when she was little, not me. She can't make me go looking for a window cleaner if I don't want to.'

'Fine. Then you're not part of this gang!' Minnie shouted.

There was a stunned silence.

Minnie bit her lip. Had she gone too far? She looked at Flora, whose eyes glistened too brightly. But she couldn't apologise, not even if Flora was upset. Sylvie had started this.

'Minnie!' Mum's voice, calling from upstairs, broke the tension. 'Is that you home? Come up now, we're going to eat.'

Everyone seemed grateful for the distraction. Minnie opened the salon door to let them out. Piotr was the last to leave. He stopped in the open doorway. 'I'm sorry your gran is frightened,' he said. 'We'll all try to make it better.

Even Sylvie.' Then he stepped into the street. The twins turned right; the boys headed left.

Minnie sighed and walked through the salon towards the stairs up to the flat.

Dad was beside the treatment room, by the broken back door. He had his toolkit and was busy unscrewing the shattered lock.

'Shouldn't you wait until the police have taken finger-prints?' she said.

He shrugged. 'There's no sign of them. And we can't leave the back door unlocked all night.'

He was right, but Minnie wondered whether the police would be cross when they arrived – it was a crime scene after all. She hoped Jimmy would be the one investigat-ing the break-in. He had helped them a lot when they'd been hunting diamonds stolen from the theatre.

She stomped up the stairs. It was weirdly quiet inside. Mum would normally have music on, old highlife tunes, or chart music – anything she could dance to while she did Sunday chores before work the next day, the loud beat battling with the roar of the Hoover. But tonight, nothing.

Minnie went into the kitchen. Mum was wiping down surfaces with spray. Something simmered gently in a pot

on the cooker. The smell of spiced meat and soft vegetables made Minnie's mouth water.

'Shall I lay the table?' Minnie asked.

'I don't know if your gran is eating with us,' Mum said.
'She seemed a bit tired. She's gone for a lie-down.'

'Oh,' Minnie said.

Mum scrubbed harder at the kitchen worktop.

'Shall I go and ask her?'

But there was no need. Gran came out of the bedroom
at that moment. Despite her bulk, she somehow managed
to look lost. It was to do with the way her shoulders
drooped, her hands clasped together. The bright, talk-
ative woman who'd got off the plane yesterday seemed
to have gone entirely. Minnie hoped that it wasn't for
good.

'No police yet?' Gran asked. Her voice shook a little.

'Not yet, Mama,' Mum said. 'We'll phone again.'

'Terrible,' Gran said. She shuffled into the kitchen and
sat down heavily in a chair.

Minnie opened the cutlery drawer as softly as she could;
the spoons chinked together despite her care. She took
out four of everything and began to lay the table.

'When will the police come?' Gran asked.

'They don't usually take this long,' Minnie said. When

they'd needed Jimmy at the theatre, he'd been there in seconds.

'It is because they think the problems of an old Nigerian woman don't matter,' Gran said.

'Our friend Jimmy won't think that. He's the local special constable,' Minnie said.

'Then where is he?' Gran said softly.

Minnie had no answer.

They heard Dad come into the flat and go to wash his hands in the bathroom. Mum took out four plates and ladled the hot stew on to them.

All through dinner they were expecting the police to call. But the phone was silent.

As Minnie got into bed that night, she could hear Gran's hands shaking as she turned the pages of her book. Gran was frightened. And the peanut boy? Where was he tonight? Was he safe?

And where was Jimmy when she needed him?

Minnie stared up at the darkness of the ceiling for a long time before she finally fell asleep.

Chapter Six

Andrew met Flora the following morning at the market. Today the traders were out and the street bustled with life. People shouted out their bargains, a chorus of special offers. Customers joked with the traders, called to each other, the business birdsong of the city.

Flora stood by the second-hand book stall. She was flicking through a plastic crate of spy thrillers when Andrew said hello.

'I've been thinking,' Flora said, without bothering with hello. 'We could try the art school to see if anyone recognises the description of the photographer. Except that it's the holidays there too, so that might not work. But maybe there'll be a caretaker or school secretary there. It's the best plan I could think of.'

Andrew shook his head. 'I've seen him before somewhere, I know it.'

'Where?' Flora asked.

Andrew shrugged. He'd been deliberately *not* thinking about it all night. He'd hoped the answer would come while he was not thinking about it, the way that sometimes the perfect comeback would pop into his head two hours after he needed it. But, despite his best efforts, the answer hadn't come.

'You need to be distracted,' Flora said, once he'd explained. She put the tattered paperback she was holding back in the box and turned to the market. 'You should recite the twelve times table, or describe the water cycle – something to keep your mind occupied while your subconscious works.'

'One times twelve is twelve,' Andrew began, 'two times twelve is twenty-four, three times twelve is … er …'

'Thirty-six.'

'I was about to say that.' They walked aimlessly, wandering past the fruit and veg stall with its smells of citrus and sunshine, past the phone stall with its bright covers in jewel colours and glitter. 'Four times twelve is forty-eight, five times twelve is … steak on rye!'

They were next to a burger van that smelled of sweet roast onions and sizzling meat.

'You can't even concentrate on being distracted,' Flora said sadly.

'No! Steak on rye! I remember where I've seen the photographer!' Andrew grabbed Flora's arm with glee. 'Remember when I trailed Albie in the theatre mystery? Well, he went to buy lunch and he walked past a gallery! I saw the man inside.'

'Are you sure? It was ages ago now.'

'I'm sure! It was just a glimpse, but I'm sure it was the photographer.'

'What should we do?'

Andrew laughed. 'We go and investigate, of course!'

He practically ran all the way to the gallery. It was opposite the Theatre Grand, where Hollywood actress, Betty Massino, had had her necklace stolen. There was a steak grill house on the street, with some metal tables outside. It was too early for lunch customers yet, so the tables were empty. The gallery was near the grill house, beside a dry cleaner's. Its facade was painted bright white, with the name painted in a matt white above the door – *Ikonik*. You could only see the name from certain angles. There was a big glass window at the front of the shop with a ... Andrew wasn't at all sure what it was: a something made of brown clumps of metal in pride of place.

'Is it meant to be a dog maybe?' Flora asked, looking at the window display.

Andrew shrugged. 'I thought it was meant to be a table.'

'Definitely something with four legs,' Flora agreed.

Andrew opened the door carefully. A tiny bell jangled above his head.

More white. White walls, white ceiling, white tiled floor. At the back was a white counter which blended into the walls.

It wasn't the sort of shop that felt like a shop.

'I'll be right there!' a man's voice called from somewhere out back.

Flora stepped over to look at the art on the walls. Some of it was paintings, swirls of colour in thick brushstrokes, red and gold and orange. But some of it was sculpture, like the something in the window. Flora had been to a big gallery and museum with school once, and there had been huge paintings of ships at sea, and people in pouffy dresses and frilly coats standing by trees. The school had had to fill in a worksheet about perspective.

The art here was nothing like that.

There was a sheet made of hammered gold ingots hanging on the wall, but when she looked closer she saw

49

they were actually bottle tops pierced and sewn together. Another wall had a series of faces, like masks, hung on it, but they were made from empty plastic bottles. Who was making art out of rubbish? If it were her, she'd have rinsed it and chucked it in the recycling.

Some of the pieces were block prints, one shape repeated over and over like patterned curtains. She didn't mind the fish one: it would make a nice duvet cover.

Then she noticed the white labels beside each object. With prices on them. Flora gasped – she had no idea people paid so much money for old bottles and potato print fish!

'I like this one,' Andrew said.

'An excellent choice,' a voice said.

Flora turned: it was the photographer. She recognised him from Lowdog-Michael's phone. He was still wearing the cream suit with the spotted bow tie. His white hair tufted up in all directions. He smiled vaguely at them. He reminded Flora of the kindly uncle in children's books.

She felt herself blush. It seemed mean to treat him like a suspect.

'It's late twentieth century,' the man said. He was talking about the print that Andrew liked: green and blue waves with a red fishing boat riding the crest.

'Is it the most expensive one here?' Andrew asked.

The man chuckled. 'I said it was an excellent choice; I didn't say it was our most expensive piece. Do you think the price of a work of art reflects its value?'

Andrew, who had never thought about the value of art before, was lost for words – for about two seconds. 'Well, if lots of people want it, and there's only one like it in the whole world, then the price will go up. And if lots of people want it, then it must be good,' he said.

'Well said. And are you in the market for art?'

Andrew shook his head ruefully. 'No, sorry. I've never been in a gallery before. Is it all right that we just came in?'

'It's a pleasure to have you. As you can see, I'm sadly not over-run with customers today. Perhaps I can offer you some refreshment? I have lemonade – shop bought, but very nice.'

They both nodded.

The man brought his heels together in a funny salute, then he disappeared out the back of the shop.

'I don't think it can have been him,' Andrew hissed.

Flora understood at once – the gallery owner didn't seem a likely candidate for stealing the suitcase from Minnie's flat. Or for using index fingers to cast spells. Still, he might have seen something or heard something that would help.

'We have to find out what he was doing in the alley,' she said.

The man was back quickly, with a tray holding three tall glasses of sparkling lemonade; ice cubes clinked as he put the tray on the counter.

'I'm sure you are both as supremely graceful as swans in flight,' he said, 'but I'd appreciate it if you stayed away from the exhibits while you drink.'

They went to join him.

The counter was almost empty. A wire tray – also white – held paperwork, A4 letters and bills. A white ceramic pot held some pencils. A red stapler was the only splash of colour.

'Delicious, thank you,' Flora said softly as she took a sip. She put her glass back on the tray. It didn't seem likely that a photographer, a gallery owner, would want to steal a suitcase of boys' clothes. She wondered how they could ask about the alley. But Andrew got there first.

'My friend saw you in an alleyway yesterday. Photographing a wall.'

'Did he? Well, yes, I have an interest in recording liminal boundaries and the conjunction of materials on vertical planes.'

'What?'

'Brick walls. I like to photograph brick walls.'

Flora had to stop herself giggling. *Walls?* Who photographed walls?

'They are fascinating,' the man said. 'They divide people, allocate land; bricks are made from fired earth – land itself used to demarcate land.'

Andrew, who was evidently no longer listening, took a gulp of lemonade, emptied the glass and burped.

Flora blushed again.

'Excuse me,' Andrew said with a grin.

'You are excused,' the man said. 'Bubbles have that effect on me too sometimes.'

'Was it good? The alleyway? Could we see the photos you took?' Andrew asked.

The man frowned, as if troubled by a bit of building gas himself. 'There was a fine example of Ruabon Red brick, as I recall. But I haven't been through the shots yet. They are far from ready for the eyes of an audience.'

'I'm not bothered about the bricks,' Andrew said. 'There was a burglary that happened around there and you might have photographed a valuable clue without even knowing it.'

The photographer turned a shade of puce.

Flora stepped in. 'I'm sure the bricks were very interesting too,' she said. 'And we'd love to know more about the Ruabon Red. But, primarily, we'd be interested to know whether there was anyone else nearby. Anything suspicious at all, you see.'

The photographer looked as though he was struggling to stay calm. Not looking at Andrew seemed to help. 'There were some very irritating boys on a bench. One of them appeared to be attempting to dislocate his own arms. But I saw no one else.'

Oh.

Flora couldn't help feeling disappointed that he couldn't give them any new leads. But at least they'd got some nice lemonade out of their enquiries.

'We'd better go,' she said. With any luck, one of the others would have found out more.

'I realise I haven't had the pleasure of making your acquaintance properly,' the man said. 'I'm Marcus Mainwaring.' He held out his hand.

'Flora Hampshire,' Flora said.

'Andrew Graham Thomas Jones,' Andrew said.

'Well, I hope to meet you again sometime, I really do,' Marcus said with a tight smile.

Chapter Seven

Sylvie was alone. All around her the market bustled with movement: prams cut up the walkways, bags swung with watermelons and cantaloupes big enough to crack her head if she wasn't careful. But despite all the people, Sylvie was on her own.

Fine. That was just the way she wanted it anyway. She didn't want to be with the others. They were all boring and stupid. She didn't need them.

There was something in her eye. She rubbed it quickly.

It was a short stomp through the noisy market to the cafe. She kept her head down and avoided low-swinging fruit dangers.

The cafe door was propped open to let in the cooler air. The smell of frying bacon and sausage and eggs made Sylvie's stomach rumble. She managed not to scowl at Eileen, the cafe owner.

'What's up with you?' Eileen asked. 'You've a face like a sunken battleship.'

'Nothing.'

'Cookie?'

'Yes, please.'

'On the house. Which means it's free. Now let's see if that makes you crack a smile.'

Sylvie smiled in spite of herself. But her face dropped again like a slamming drawbridge when she remembered she was here for more than excellent cookies. 'Eileen, did your window cleaner come yesterday?'

'Old Derek? Yes, he likes to come on a Sunday when the market isn't here. And when there are no customers. And when I'm not here. He doesn't like people very much, you see.'

Eileen put a chocolate chip cookie the size of her hand on to a gleaming white side plate and pushed it across the counter. 'Why?' she asked. 'Your mum need a window cleaner, does she?'

Sylvie picked up the plate with both hands. The gooey chocolate smelled delicious. It made her feel a teensy bit better. 'No. It's for a case.'

Eileen's eyes widened. She'd been so impressed by their last case, she'd cut out the story from the local paper and pinned it to the cafe wall, next to her food hygiene certificate and a photo of her cat. 'Well, if you're investigating, I'll write down his number. He's not a suspect, is he? He'd not hurt a fly. Though he has been known to take against humans every now and then. Here.' Eileen scribbled something on her waitressing pad, tore it off and handed it to Sylvie. It was Derek's phone number. 'Although,' Eileen continued, 'he usually likes to come in for a pork pie around ten-ish, so you could just wait if you wanted.'

Sylvie looked at the scrap of paper. She could call Derek and try to get him to talk. But she'd probably get more out of him if she saw him in person. And she needed to get *something* useful out of him. She couldn't go back to the gang empty-handed. Minnie would raise an eyebrow and look smug, and Piotr would look sorry for her. Flora and Andrew probably wouldn't say anything, but they'd be *thinking* that she was useless. And Sylvie Hampshire was a lot of things, but useless wasn't one of them.

She was going to stay and wait for Derek.

Sylvie carried the huge cookie to an empty table and sat down to wait. She broke off tiny chunks and nibbled at them hamster-style. She kept a close eye on the open doorway – families came in, traders, young couples, no window cleaners. She was just hoovering up the very last few cookie crumbs with a damp fingertip when Eileen gave her a low whistle and nodded towards a man who'd just walked in.

He was stooped, with knees that pointed apart like a signpost. He wore overalls that had once been white, but were now the same dirty grey colour as his hair. He collected a pie on a plate from the counter without saying a word, then sat down, with his back towards the room.

Sylvie abandoned her empty plate on the table and made her way over. 'Do you mind if I sit here?' she asked.

The man grunted. It could have been 'yes', it could have been 'no', it could have been, 'Clear off before I call the police.' It was hard to tell. Sylvie sat down.

'You're a window cleaner,' she said. It was only now that she wished she'd spent her waiting time thinking of clever ways to find out what Derek knew. But she hadn't.

Derek grunted again.

'I'd like to be a window cleaner,' Sylvie tried desperately. 'Fresh air, interesting clients, er, clean glass.'

Derek looked up slowly. His dark eyes locked on her. 'I'm eating,' he said slowly. 'Be quiet.' He took a bite of his pie; flakes of pastry stuck to his chin.

Sylvie sniffed. She sat on her hands. She looked out of the window.

Then she looked back at Derek.

'Look,' she said. 'I'll be quiet and I'll even go away if you answer *one* question.'

Derek looked wary. 'What?'

'I think you were in the alley by the side of this cafe yesterday. This isn't the one question by the way, this is me leading up to my one question. I think you were in the alley yesterday morning while something strange was happening nearby. This is the question now: did you see anyone break into the salon next door? Oh, and a supplementary question, which perhaps should have been my real question, so I'm making it my question: did you break into the salon?'

Derek's wrinkled weather-worn face changed colour. The grey gave way to red, then burgundy. 'What?' he yelled.

'You can't answer my question with a question, that's not fair,' Sylvie said.

'How dare you? I came in here to eat a pie and I get accused by some little slip of a thing! My old dad didn't fight in the war so that I could be insulted by girls!' A fine mist of spittle mixed with puff pastry particles sprayed over the plastic tabletop.

'Sorry, I didn't mean –'

'Clear off. Go on. I won't have this. Go on!'

Sylvie stood up quickly, banging her knee on the table leg. The sudden pain made her eyes water. It wasn't the horrible man shouting at her. Definitely not.

'Hey, Derek.' Eileen was by the table. 'It's all right.'

'No, no, it isn't! This girl is a pest, a nuisance … a pestilential infestation of the highest order.'

Eileen smiled. 'I wouldn't go that far.'

Eileen had smiled! Sylvie couldn't believe it. This man was shouting at her, insulting her, and Eileen pretty much agreed with him! She felt a solid lump in her throat, like a cough sweet lodged there. She could feel tears on her cheeks now. This was awful!

Sylvie covered her face, turned and stumbled out of the cafe into the street.

They'd been horrible to her! They'd all been horrible – Derek, Eileen, even Flora and Andrew and Piotr.

And it was all Minnie's fault.

Chapter Eight

Minnie met Piotr in the small play park outside his block of flats. She had her phone ready, and she'd printed off a list of dry cleaners. There were quite a lot. 'I had no idea so many people don't do their own laundry,' Minnie said in amazement.

Piotr twirled on the swing with one foot on the ground as a pivot, so that the chain twisted and twisted. When he lifted his foot, he whipped back in the other direction.

'Piotr! You have to take this seriously!' It was bad enough that Sylvie wasn't doing much to help.

Piotr gave a slow grin. 'I am. I was thinking about this last night.'

'What? What is it?' He clearly had something to tell her.

He paused. Then, seeing that he was about to get a thump on the arm if he didn't speak, he said, 'It's that baseball cap. The one that Lowdog and Gnasher loved so much.'

'Yeah?'

'It had an ace of spades on it. What if that wasn't just any old symbol? What if it was the logo of the company?'

Minnie frowned. 'I don't know. This list doesn't have the logos on. We'd have to go back to mine and look at the internet. If you're wrong, it would waste a lot of time. Time the boy from Lagos might not have.' She had dreamed about juju knives last night; it wasn't something she wanted to do again.

Piotr stopped the swing and leaped off. 'We don't need to do that. Think about it. Ace. A.C.E.?'

Minnie frowned, shrugged.

'We walked right past it the other day on the way to church! Ahmed's Cleaning Experts!'

Minnie squealed. Of course they had! 'Why are we still here then?' she said. 'We've got a suspect to interview!'

The park was abandoned. They raced away, Minnie letting herself sprint as fast as she could, with Piotr close behind. The air whipped at her plaits and pressed her T-shirt flat against her skin. The market was an obstacle course of crates and cardboard boxes to hurdle over, pedestrians to dodge, stalls to weave between.

Ahmed's Cleaning Experts was beside the theatre square. They slowed and stopped, pausing to catch their breath. Minnie grinned. 'Beat you,' she managed to say between gasps.

'Only because,' Piotr wheezed, 'I wasn't trying.'

She pushed open the door to the shop. The first thing she noticed was the smell – a kind of harsh chemical one, a bit like the swimming baths, fighting with the floral pong of potpourri. Then the shape of the shop: a counter cut across the narrow width of the room, close to the front door. Behind the counter, a man. He had dark hair, black-brown eyes. His skin was light brown. He wore a white coat, like a doctor or dentist. The name badge on his coat said 'Omar'. He didn't smile as they walked in.

He looked as though he were guarding the rest of the shop.

Behind him, long racks of clothes stretched along the side walls. One rack looked like ghosts suspended from a scaffold – every hanger was draped in a white plastic bag. The other rack must have been for the dirty clothes, as they had no bags; they were just on hangers with paper labels clipped to the wire: at the front end, a green T-shirt with a logo, then a long pink and purple silk dress, followed by sombre black suits, thick brown and tan fur coats and floating cream and white chiffon gowns. Beautiful clothes.

Minnie took in everything in an instant. Then she looked at the man, Omar.

His eyes flicked behind them, obviously waiting for a grown-up to follow them inside.

Minnie gave him her widest smile.

'Can I help you?' Omar said. His voice was frostier than a husky's toes.

'I hope so,' Minnie said brightly. 'I'm doing a summer holiday project for school on the best industries to work in. I wonder if I could ask you a few questions?'

'I'm busy,' Omar said.

'It won't take two minutes. What do you like best about your job?'

Omar shrugged. 'I get paid. It is important to be paid.'

'What about the worst bits? For example, what are the hours like? Do you have to work weekends?'

'We clean every day. Every day except Sunday,' Omar said.

'And you do deliveries of clothes?'

'For regular customers only,' Omar replied.

'On Sundays?' Minnie asked.

'Sometimes. Why is this question in your project?'

Minnie smiled again. Omar was as friendly as a wasp with a parking ticket, but that didn't mean she was ready to give up.

'We have to decide what job we'd like to do when we grow up. I like clothes. If I can't be a fashion designer, maybe I can clean clothes. But I don't want to work on Sundays. My family go to church on Sundays, you see.'

She watched him carefully as she spoke. Was that a flicker of fear on his face? Of recognition?

Piotr stepped up to the counter. 'Do you work here by yourself? What about Mr Ahmed? Could we interview him?'

Omar folded his arms. His strong-looking, thick arms. 'There is no Ahmed. I called the shop Ahmed's so I would come top of the list in the directory. There is only me.'

'Oh,' Piotr said. 'Would you mind if we took a picture? For the cover of our project?'

Omar shook his head. 'No, you certainly may not. You are very annoying to me now,' he said in disgust. 'I have no idea why my mother is so sad not to have grandchildren. Children are more trouble than verrucas. I will ask you to leave now. I do not want to be in your project.'

Piotr glanced at Minnie. He looked frustrated, his brow creased.

She gave him a quick wink. 'Thank you, Mr Omar,' Minnie said brightly. 'You've been very helpful.'

She tugged at Piotr's arm as she headed for the door. He stumbled a little, but followed behind her. Outside, in the fresh air, Minnie checked the road before dashing across to the shade of the plane trees. She threw herself down on to a bench with a triumphant yelp.

'What?' Piotr asked. 'Why did you thank him? He was worse than useless.'

'Was he?' Now it was Minnie's turn to grin smugly.

Piotr noticed right away. He sat down beside her. 'What did you see?'

'Did you notice anything about the clothes waiting to be cleaned?' she asked.

Piotr looked thoughtful, mentally trying to recreate the shop. 'I don't know. Fancy. Expensive. I think some of them might even have been animals once. Oh!' He grinned too. 'Except the T-shirt!'

'Exactly, a small green T-shirt with a crocodile logo! One that looked as though it could have been bought in the exact same place as the orange T-shirt in the suitcase.'

Minnie could picture the scene. The heat of Lagos, the sound of traffic roaring in the background. A boy, excited by his upcoming trip, being taken to a stallholder in a covered arcade. Cheap cotton T-shirts piled high on the tabletop, higher even than the boy's head. He'd have watched as someone, an older someone, held the T-shirt against his chest. Finding one that fit. Buying three, haggling over the price. Was the boy excited to see his new clothes? Was he looking forward to his journey? Or was he frightened by what was to come?

Minnie shivered.

Yes, Gran was scared, and yes, the flat felt weird, but somewhere there was a boy who was living with the people who had done that. People who cut the eyes from boys in postcards, who made her dream of knives.

That boy needed their help.

Chapter Nine

Minnie and Piotr walked back to the cafe and went to sit at their usual table.

Minnie felt a worried fizzing inside: it was the same way she felt before tests. How were they going to help the boy from Lagos?

Bam!

A slap on the window made her jump.

Andrew.

He pressed his mouth up against the glass and blew. His cheeks ballooned out like some deep-sea fish.

'Oi!' Eileen shouted from behind the counter. 'You're smearing the clean window.'

Andrew stopped smearing the window and wiped it with his sleeve.

Gross.

Seconds later, he was inside the cafe and at the table.

'Flora just went home for a minute. She's got something she wants to show us,' he said.

'What?' Piotr asked.

Andrew shrugged. 'We found the photographer – he's an art dealer. Some of the paintings in his shop are worth an absolute fortune! But some of them look like they were painted by a class of Year Ones who've eaten too much Haribo, so I wasn't that impressed.'

'Did he say anything about the burglary?' Piotr asked.

'No. He didn't see anything except for some pretty excellent bricks.'

'Bricks?'

Minnie couldn't ask him any more, because Flora walked in. She was already rooting in her backpack. She pulled out her notebook. When she sat down, it was open on a blank page, ready to take notes. 'What did you find out about the dry cleaner?' she asked. Her voice sounded strange, tight and high.

'What's the matter?' Minnie said. 'Where's Sylvie?'

Flora flushed an immediate, violent pink. 'Well, that's the thing. You see. So I saw Sylvie at home. And the thing is …'

'Spit it out.'

'I'm sorry, but Sylvie won't come back until you apologise to her.'

Minnie's mouth goldfished in astonishment. 'Me? Why does she want me to say sorry? What for?'

'Derek the window cleaner. She thinks you did it deliberately.'

'Did what?' Minnie's fists curled in her lap.

'Sent her on her own to be insulted.' Flora sounded forlorn. 'Sorry,' she added.

'It's not your fault. But it isn't mine either! I don't care if Sylvie comes back or not. As if I'm going to say sorry.' How dare Sylvie? It was as though the whole world revolved around her. Well, not Minnie. No one told her what to do. Unless they were related to her.

'Well,' Flora said. 'I'm just passing on the message.'

'We know,' Piotr said gently. 'It's really not your fault.' From his tone, it was hard to work out whose fault he thought it was.

'Did she tell you what Derek told her?' Andrew asked.

'She said he was worse than useless. He just got upset. Did you have any luck with the dry cleaner?' It was obvious that Flora was changing the subject. Minnie was willing to let her, though she was still fuming at Sylvie.

It didn't take long for Piotr to tell them all about Omar and the green T-shirt.

They sat in silence for a moment, thinking about the little boy.

Then Flora pulled something out of her notebook. It was a replica she'd made of the postcard. The boys near the sea. 'I think it's the right size,' Flora said. 'I put your photo through postcard-making software. Does this look the same?'

Minnie took it. It was a bit thinner, a bit lighter than the original, but otherwise it was a perfect copy. Flora had even cut out squares where the holes had been. 'It's amazing,' Minnie said.

Piotr took it. 'It is really weird. Creepy,' he said. 'No wonder you didn't like it. What sort of magic is it for, do you think?'

'Bad magic,' Minnie said. 'My second cousin, Temi, said witches put curses on enemies to make them die.'

Flora pressed down the centre of her notebook, ironing out the spine with a *crack*. She held her pen tightly, her fingertips bone pale. 'Omar is suspect number one,' Flora said as she wrote his name at the top of the page. 'How do we find out if he's hiding a little boy against his will?'

'Stake-out,' Andrew said. 'We need to creep in under cover of darkness, search every inch of the dry cleaner's and use our deadly ninja skills to find him.'

'Oh, yes.' Minnie raised her eyes to the ceiling. 'Our deadly ninja skills. Silly me. I'd forgotten about those.'

'Maybe we won't break in,' Piotr said. 'I'd prefer not to break the law if we don't have to. But we can definitely watch the shop, see if anyone goes in or out. Watch for anything suspicious.'

'We'll have to take shifts,' Andrew said. 'Five kids standing outside staring at the shop? He'll know we're on to him.'

'Four kids,' Flora said forlornly.

'*Pff,*' Minnie said, not wanting to think about Sylvie just now. Or ever.

'OK,' Piotr said, 'me and Andrew can take the first shift. Minnie and Flora take over in an hour. All right?'

Flora didn't reply. She didn't move. Her pen hovered in mid-air, pointing. She was stock-still, almost bristling, like a terrier about to chase a cat.

'Are you OK?' Minnie asked.

Flora gestured with her pen, pointing at the table.

The grey plastic wipe-clean surface was the same as it ever was. Salt, pepper, sachets of sugar. Normal.

A laminated menu smeared in places with dried-on mustard. The postcard thrown down on top of it.

All normal.

Then Minnie saw what Flora could see.

Where the postcard overlaid the menu, the empty cut-outs framed certain letters beneath: 'gs', 'au', 'ra', 'ak' – parts of words where eyes should be. The postcard was highlighting letters!

'A cipher,' Flora whispered.

'What?' Piotr asked.

'A cipher is a code, a way to send a hidden message. The boy was carrying the cipher to someone who needed to read a hidden message. You have to send the cipher and the message separately because if they get intercepted, it's too easy to decode. He was delivering the cipher.'

He was a delivery boy? Not a walking larder of curse ingredients? The relief was like a wave crashing over Minnie. He was going to keep all his fingers. But the feeling didn't last long. Only criminals would need ciphers smuggled across borders. A shiver caterpillared up her spine. The boy was being used by criminals. Minnie leaned forwards, her elbows on the table. 'What's it for?' she asked. 'What does it decode?'

Flora looked up from her notebook, where she was scribbling furiously. 'I have no idea. There must be a message somewhere. A letter or a flyer. It could be anything!'

Glances passed around the table like a relay baton, each person wondering if the others had any bright ideas. No one did.

Minnie picked up the replica postcard and flipped it between her fingers. Flora had done such a good job, she'd even printed the back of the original.

The back!

Minnie laid the postcard down with a wide grin and stabbed at it with her index finger. 'Post in two days!' she said.

'What?' Andrew asked.

'Post in two days! That's where the hidden message is. The boy was supposed to deliver this by hand, then the letter would follow in two days. Just in the regular post. I mean, if the secret message is hidden, then it can be delivered by the postman and no one would ever even know it's there.'

'Hiding in plain sight,' Flora whispered.

'Minnie, you're a genius!' Piotr said.

'So,' Andrew said, 'the ninja stake-out needs to watch for suspicious people and suspicious post. Got it.'

Minnie wasn't sure what to do with herself for an hour while she waited for her turn to keep watch. She felt as though she had energy zipping right down to the tips of her toes. She left the cafe and bounced into the salon. Bernice, Mum's assistant, was looking harassed. Her face glistened with sweat, and patches had formed under her arms. She ran between three customers, plaiting and weaving and braiding hair like a machine. A sweaty machine.

'Where's Mum?' Minnie asked.

'An excellent question,' Bernice said. 'If you could find her and ask her to come and take care of her one o'clock appointment, that way I might not hand in my resignation.'

'OK,' Minnie said. It wasn't like Mum to forget an appointment. She raced up the stairs to the flat. 'Mum? Mum!' she called.

Mum didn't reply, but she could hear her voice. And Dad's. They were speaking softly, but with a crisp tone, like swirling autumn leaves. Minnie crept to the kitchen, where the voices were coming from.

'There is nothing wrong with keeping eggs in a cupboard,' Mum was saying. 'They don't need to be in a fridge.'

'I know that,' Dad said.

'So why has she moved them?'

Eggs? Were they really cross about eggs?

'She's just trying to help,' Dad said. 'Listen, I have to go to work now. So do you. We can talk about this later.'

Dad turned and saw Minnie in the hallway. A pained look flashed across his face, then it was gone and he gave her a sad smile. 'See if you can entertain Gran, will you? That might stop her grocery stealth tactics.'

Mum didn't say goodbye to Dad as he left. She stood at the sink with her back to the rest of the kitchen. 'Why does everything have to be such a drama?' she said, a bit too loudly.

Minnie didn't know what to do. She'd hardly ever heard her parents raise their voices at each other. She dithered in the hall. Then she remembered that Dad had asked her to take care of Gran, so she went to look for her.

She found Gran in their bedroom. Her bedclothes were smoothed and wrinkle free, despite the fact that Gran was forced to sit on the bed. She was dressed, with her hair done, her coat on and her handbag clasped in her lap. It looked as though she was intending to go somewhere.

As soon as Minnie stepped into the room, Gran spoke.

'Drama, eh? I'm making drama? That's what your mother believes? Three days I've been here and already

I've lost my belongings, we've been burgled, the police have taken no interest, and it's me creating drama? This place is worse than a Nollywood home video. I moved some eggs. Is that a crime, eh?'

Minnie *really* couldn't believe that the grown-ups were arguing over eggs.

Gran stood abruptly. 'Well, I've had enough,' she said. 'If Mohammad cannot go to the mountain, then the mountain must come to Mohammad. And you're coming with me.'

'Where are we going?'

'To find someone who will take me seriously.'

Gran marched past Minnie out into the hallway and towards the front door. Minnie trotted after her. Before she left the flat, she glanced back and yelled to Mum, 'Bernice says please remember your one o'clock appointment.'

Gran was down the stairs before Minnie caught up with her. She clutched her sensible brown handbag like a shield before all enemies and stalked out of the salon without glancing at Bernice or the customers. Minnie scurried in her wake.

Gran stuttered to a halt in the street, her righteous indignation failing for a moment. She looked right, then left. 'Which way is it to the police station?' she asked.

For one wild moment, Minnie wondered whether Gran was going to have Mum arrested for poor egg storage. Then she realised that Gran was taking a report of the break-in to the police, instead of waiting for the police to come to her. The mountain going to Mohammad.

'We go right here, then left by the theatre,' she said. She had never had any reason to go into the police station, but passed by it on the way to school.

Gran headed off with such determined strides that she looked more like a warrior than a pensioner.

As they stalked through the square, Minnie glanced at the dry cleaner's. And the bench. Andrew and Piotr were sitting on it. Ninja stake-out. But she had no time to stop and talk to them; Gran charged forwards like a warship heading into battle.

The police station was a low-rise concrete building, mostly ash grey and mottled brown. It had the look of a multi-storey car park with low-level depression. A blue sign above the door said 'POLICE'. Gran didn't even pause for breath before pushing open the scuffed door and marching over to reception.

Gran was going to pick a fight with the police! Minnie felt her fizzing excitement overflow. Gran was cool!

'I want to talk to whoever is in charge,' Gran said.

The man behind the desk was white and alarmed. He wore a dark uniform and his long fingers were already reaching for a pen and clipboard.

'Did you hear me?' Gran said. 'The boss man, right now.'

'Well,' the officer replied, 'our police commissioner is a woman. But I don't expect she can see you without an appointment, Mrs ... ?' He trailed off, waiting for Gran to give her name.

'Mrs Adesina. I am not going anywhere until I have given this boss woman a piece of my mind. The way I have been treated is disgraceful!'

He scrawled something quickly at the top of the clipboard. Then something else. Then he crossed that out and looked up. 'Could you please tell me the nature of your complaint?'

Gran heaved in a heavy breath. She pulled her handbag up to her chest. She fixed needle sharp eyes on the officer. 'Are you the police commissioner?' she asked with a bass rumble.

The officer quailed. 'No,' he said.

'Then I will thank you for not wasting my time. *Get me the commissioner.*'

Gran was formidable.

The officer put down his pen and reached for the phone. He spoke quickly to someone, then was transferred to another someone. He told whoever was on the other end that Mrs Adesina was most insistent, but no, had no appointment; he paused, waited, wavered. Then he looked shocked: his eyebrows almost hit his hairline. 'Really? What, now? No, of course, right away.'

He put the phone down gently, as though it were made of glass. 'She says she'll see you,' he whispered in amazement. 'Follow me.'

He buzzed them through a door beyond reception. They were in a small corridor painted a watery blue that was clearly meant to say 'stay calm' but made Minnie think of hospitals and secondary schools and other panicky places.

The officer appeared beside them. 'This way,' he said as he led them past closed doors with black and white nameplates, rows of tired-looking chairs, noticeboards with sheets of paper pinned on top of each other in bureaucratic petals. Gran stayed silent.

They came to a closed door with 'Police Commissioner Anthea Swift' written on it. The officer rapped smartly. When the reply 'Come!' came, he opened the door and ushered them inside.

The police commissioner stood up from her desk. She smiled warmly and held out an elegant, French-manicured hand. Minnie briefly admired the quality of the work. Her dark hair fell in a neat bob; a ribbon of silver grey ran through her fringe like a badger's stripe. Classy. Definitely classy.

'Mrs Adesina,' she said. 'Please, call me Anthea.' She took Gran's hand, wrapping both of hers around the shake. 'Do, please, sit.' Anthea waved towards two chairs set in front of her desk. They were much more vibrant than the corridor ones. These were cerise pink, with velvet buttons decorating the back. Gran settled into hers like a Dobermann taking guard.

Anthea winced as the expensive-looking chair creaked.

'My son,' Gran began, 'called the police yesterday to report a break-in. And no one has so much as looked in our direction. It's not good enough! This wouldn't happen in Lagos!'

Anthea sat back into her chair on the other side of the desk. 'You're from Lagos? Such an exciting city, a great mix of old and new.'

'Don't try to divert me with your sugar-tongue flattery! What I want is police work!'

81

Anthea reddened. 'Yes, of course. Let me just see ... Adesina.' She tapped at a tiny laptop, which was the only clutter on her desk. She frowned. 'Oh dear,' she said. 'I'm afraid there was a clerical error. The case was marked 'Concluded'. I'm so sorry for the mix-up. I'll get someone on it right away.'

'Special Constable Wright?' Minnie asked hopefully.

'Would you like that?' Anthea said.

Minnie nodded. Jimmy would do his best for Gran, she was sure of it.

'Then Jimmy Wright it will be!' Anthea tapped lightly at the keyboard, her fingers dancing across the keys. 'He'll be in touch shortly. You have my guarantee.'

The police commissioner stood up. It was clear she thought the meeting was over.

Gran laid her hands against the arm rests, clearly deciding whether to hoist herself up or not. Had Anthea done enough? Apparently, yes. Gran stood up and shook hands across the desk. 'Thank you,' Gran said. 'It is nice to be listened to for once.'

Then they were out of the office, retracing their steps.

'Now we should see some results,' Gran said with relish.

Minnie agreed. Jimmy would help them find the lost boy.

Chapter Ten

Gran swayed sedately through the police station, a victorious battleship sailing back to port. She gave a wave to the officer on desk duty. 'That,' she told Minnie, 'is how you get things done. You go straight to the top.'

Minnie thought she'd take advantage of Gran's good mood. 'I said I'd see my friends this afternoon,' she said. 'Do you think it's OK if I'm out until tea?'

'I don't see why not. I'll rearrange our bedroom while you're out. I feel I can take on anything, even that cramped room. You see your friends, especially that lovely girl Sylvie.'

Minnie wanted to say just what she thought of Sylvie and her demand for an apology – the king of Ife himself could order it, and there was still no way Minnie would say sorry! – but she bit her tongue. She'd been given permission and she did not want to rock the boat.

She gave Gran a solid kiss on her cheek. She'd been so amazing, standing up to the police commissioner, that Minnie just couldn't help herself. Gran gave a pleased grin, then waved Minnie away. 'Go on, see your friends.'

Minnie raced to the bench where Andrew and Piotr were still sitting.

'Anything happening?' Minnie asked.

Piotr shook his head. 'Nothing. Some customers. But Omar hasn't left the shop once, and there's no sign of a kid at all.'

Minnie plonked down on to the wooden slats. They were scored and magic-markered with the names of people who'd sat there before her – *Katie 4 Eva*, *JonnieBoy*, and she smiled to see *Anna 4 Lowdog*.

'You're here early,' Andrew said. 'I was hoping that I could solve this case and find the boy before you showed up. Another ten minutes would have done it, I reckon.'

Minnie rested her elbows on the back of the bench and looked at the dry cleaner's. It seemed so ordinary: a single-storey shop with a sign that had once been new and hopeful but was dusty now and faded by the sunlight; an 'OPEN' sign hanging by the door at a wonky angle. All normal, pretty much like Mum's salon.

Then she paused. 'It will have a back door, won't it?'

Piotr and Andrew looked at her.

'I mean, on the other side of the shop there'll be a back door? Like at the salon.'

'You think we're watching the wrong door?' Piotr asked.

'I think we're watching the wrong door,' Minnie agreed.

'How do we get around the back?'

There was no obvious alleyway that would lead there, no path or side street.

'Perhaps you can only get to it through the shop?' Andrew suggested.

'Well then,' Piotr said, 'that's the end of that. We can hardly go into the dry cleaner's and ask Omar if we can go through the shop so that we can spy on him.' He toed a hollow of dirt underneath the bench, kicking up a mini sandstorm in disgust.

'No,' Andrew said. 'But we could go through Marcus's shop next door. Marcus is the gallery owner. He was really nice yesterday. I bet he'd say we could.'

Minnie felt a sparrow flutter of excitement. The gallery was right next door to the dry cleaner's; their backyards must be right next to each other. They would probably be able to see inside the back of the dry cleaner's from the gallery's yard. The boy might even be standing at the window!

She leaped up from the bench. 'Come on, Andrew, time for you to be charming.'

Andrew stood and gave an elaborate bow. 'At your service,' he said.

'I'll wait here' – Piotr hadn't moved – 'just in case anyone does come to the front door to see Omar.'

Minnie and Andrew left Piotr on watch duty. They crossed the road carefully, nipping between cyclists and cars.

'Are you sure he's nice?' Minnie said, with one hand on the gallery door handle.

'I'm sure,' Andrew said, and gave her a gentle nudge. The door opened and they were both standing inside.

'Andrew!' a warm voice said. 'The art lover returns. And brings another acolyte to the altar of Apollo.'

'You what?' Andrew said.

Marcus spread his arms wide before Minnie and urged her into the shop. 'Forgive me. I mean to say that you have returned with another young lady who may also come to love the arts.'

Andrew still looked a little confused. 'Er, Marcus, this is Minnie. Minnie, Marcus.'

'Hello,' she said. She didn't think she'd ever met anyone quite like Marcus. His suit was crease free and elegant; his bow tie looked as though Marcus had actually tied it, not like the clip-on one Dad had worn to Bernice's wedding.

'Although it is a pleasure, of course, I didn't expect to see you again so soon,' Marcus said. 'What brings you to my neck of the diminutive forest?'

'The diminted ... ?'

'The woods. What brings you to my neck of the woods?'

'A mission,' Andrew said.

'How enthralling!' Marcus looked at Minnie more shrewdly than she expected. 'We must feed the imagination, don't you think?' he stage-whispered to her. 'I sense that Andrew has a very vivid imagination. I too am given to wild ideas. You seem to have your feet more firmly on the ground.'

Was Marcus insulting Andrew? She glanced at Andrew, just to check, but Andrew didn't look at all offended. He was grinning proudly. If he had a very vivid imagination, then he was pleased about it.

'When you've got size six feet,' Minnie replied, 'it's difficult to get them off the ground.'

Marcus laughed. 'You're a tonic,' he said. 'Let me bring you both a drink and you can tell me all about the "mission".' He did stupid air quotes with his hands. Minnie decided she didn't like him.

Marcus's body was all angles, but he moved gracefully, like a heron, as he went to the back of the shop. Minnie and Andrew were left alone beside the counter.

'I don't think we should tell him why we're really here,' Minnie hissed.

'Why not? He'll help us,' Andrew said.

She shook her head vigorously. As she did, her eyes caught sight of something on the desk. Something very, very odd. She felt a tingle spread from her tummy out to her arms and legs. She wanted to yelp, but forced herself to be quiet.

In the wire tray was a cream-coloured envelope. The address of the gallery was handwritten. The thing that made Minnie stifle a yelp were the stamps. There were three of them in the top right-hand corner – a smiling black girl stood against an orange and blue background. In bold letters, the stamps were marked 'Nigeria ₦50'.

It was a letter from Nigeria.

Perhaps it was nothing. Perhaps it was just a letter from a pen pal. Or maybe a bill from a Nigerian artist.

But maybe it wasn't.

Maybe a letter arriving from Nigeria the day after a Nigerian suitcase had been stolen from her flat and a Nigerian boy was missing was too much of a coincidence to ignore.

'Andrew,' Minnie said, 'we're going to need a distraction.'

Chapter Eleven

'What sort of a distraction?' Andrew asked.

'One that keeps Marcus from looking at me for about thirty seconds,' Minnie replied.

Attracting the attention of adults was one of Andrew's special skills. They seemed to notice him even when he wasn't doing anything at all. At school the teachers would often ask what he was up to in suspicious voices when all he was doing was quietly doodling in his workbook or innocently staring out at seagulls.

He was pretty sure that he could get Marcus to watch him while Minnie did whatever it was that Minnie wanted to do.

Marcus was back in the room, carrying his neat little tray again.

Andrew was also sure that trays of drinks and expensive art didn't go together.

He stepped forward eagerly. 'Let me help you with that.'

'No, it's fine, I've got it.'

'Please. You've been so nice. I'll just take it and –'

'No, honestly, it's –'

'Right. I've got it. Where should I put it? On this stand?'

'No, no, Andrew, that's a plinth. And it's already got a sculpture on it.'

'That's all right. I can hold the tray with one hand and lift the statue off.'

'No!'

'Look, it comes right off. Should I put it on the floor, do you think? It's quite heavy. What's it made of? Pottery? We did pottery in school once. Well, not me. I just had to watch. I broke my pot right at the beginning and there wasn't time to make a second one. This really *is* heavy. I wonder how long I can hold it in one hand.'

'Andrew!' Marcus yelled. 'Put the statue back right this minute!'

'Oh. Oh, I'm sorry, you should have just said.'

Andrew put the ceramic head back exactly where he had found it. He eased it a millimetre to the left, then a hair's breadth to the right. He held the tray all the while, perfectly balanced, on his left hand. He'd had a lot of experience holding trays for Mum.

He glanced over at Minnie. She gave him a ghost of a nod.

Andrew held the tray with both hands and gave it back to Marcus. 'Sorry, Marcus, I was just trying to help.'

Marcus's cheeks were veined red and his eyes had a peculiar glassy sheen. It was a look Andrew had seen before on angry adults. Often.

Minnie edged across the room and took Andrew's arm. 'Sorry, but we'd better go,' she said. 'We didn't mean to cause trouble. It just sort of happens sometimes. Thanks for having us.'

As she spoke, she steered Andrew towards the door. They both gave a quick wave to the now speechless Marcus.

'What did you find?' Andrew asked as soon as they were out in the street.

'Let's get the others and I'll show you.'

Chapter Twelve

Minnie beckoned to Piotr, who was still watching the dry cleaner's. With her other hand she texted Flora. Her heart was beating fast. She wanted to get to the safety of the cafe. She kept expecting Marcus to call them back any second and demand to know what she was up to.

She broke into a sprint.

'What is it?' Andrew asked breathlessly.

'Did you see the backyard?' Piotr asked, running too.

'I'll explain when we're away from here. Come on,' Minnie insisted.

Inside the cafe, Minnie sat at the window and ducked down, watching the market to see that Marcus wasn't coming after them. There was no sign of him bobbing through the stalls. She let herself breathe again.

'Tell us what you saw,' Andrew begged.

'No, wait for Flora.'

They sat in an electric silence, looking out for the flash of red hair that meant Flora was running to meet them.

They didn't have to wait long. Flora burst into the cafe, her face flushed, panting, stray strands of hair haloed around her face.

'Did you bring it? Did it work?' Minnie asked.

'What are you talking about?' Andrew whined. 'The suspense is literally killing me.'

Minnie couldn't help but grin: Andrew looked a long way from dead. 'Marcus Mainwaring had a letter from Nigeria in his tray. While you distracted Marcus, I took the letter out of the envelope, photographed it and texted the photo to Flora.'

Flora unzipped her backpack and reached inside for her notebook. 'It didn't take long to print off the photo, scaled up to A4. I've brought it with me.'

'With the postcard?' Piotr asked.

'With the postcard,' Flora said.

She pulled two pieces of paper from her notebook. One was the replica postcard. The other, she unfolded and smoothed flat on the tabletop.

Minnie hadn't had time in the gallery to read the letter. She'd had to work fast just to get the photo and put the letter back in place.

There was a heraldic crest at the top of the page: a shield with a lion on either side. A motto was written in a scroll beneath the lions – *mens sana in corpore sano* – and below that 'St Aloysius High School' and a Lagos address. Typewritten text filled the rest of the page, which Flora read aloud:

Dear Mr Mainwaring,

I write to thank you for your continued support of St Aloysius School. Your kindness in sponsoring equipment here is reaping rewards.

Improvements have been incredible after the outbreak of flu, aggressive though it was. We have employed a permanent nurse to oversee the well-being of the children. Age seems no protection against ill health sadly.

While donations are always welcome, we are also working hard ourselves. Our 14th auction of arts is scheduled. Class G3 are upmost in their hopes of raising our highest total ever.

Together we will ensure a bright future for St Aloysius and our students.

Yours faithfully,
Hopeful Otlogetswe
Dean of School

On the face of it, it wasn't quite the confession of a criminal gang that Minnie had been hoping for. But if they were right, if the postcard was a cipher, then this letter might have a lot more to tell them.

Flora lifted the postcard, laid it on top of the letter and drew it slowly down the page. As soon as each of the empty squares framed a section of the text beneath, she froze.

'Write this down,' she told Andrew. He reached for her pen and scribbled on a napkin as she read out the text: 'le, ft, lu, gg, ag, e3, 14, au, g3, pm.'

'Oh.' Andrew sounded disappointed. 'It's just gibberish.'

Piotr grinned. 'No! No, it isn't. It's just got the gaps in the wrong places. Look.' Piotr drew his fingertip along the napkin as he read. 'Left Luggage 3, 14 Aug, 3 p.m.'

Minnie collapsed back on her seat. It really was a secret message. They'd been right. It took her breath away worse than the sprint from the gallery. There was an actual criminal gang operating in town. This was the proof. But doing what? She thought again of the orange T-shirt and the scruffy teddy in the battered black suitcase. This was real. They had to find the boy and get him away from the criminals.

'What's Left Luggage?' Andrew asked, bringing Minnie back to the moment.

'It's when you want to leave your luggage for a while,' Flora explained. 'Say you've got a few hours in a city and you don't want to carry your case around: you leave it in a Left Luggage locker. We went to Zurich last year by train and had a few hours in Paris. We left our luggage and went to the Champs-Élysées for macarons.'

If it had been Sylvie who'd said that, Minnie might have been tempted to make a sarcastic remark. But it was Flora, and she was probably on to something. So Minnie kept her sarky comments to herself – with a bit of a struggle. 'So you get Left Luggage at a railway station?' Minnie asked.

Flora nodded eagerly.

'Is there one at the railway station in town?' Andrew asked.

There was a collective round of shrugging and head shaking – no one knew.

'What's the date today?' Piotr asked. Without being at school, where the date would always be up on the white-board at the front of the class, they'd forgotten all about dates and days of the week.

Except Flora. 'It's the 13th today,' she said.

97

'Well, then,' Piotr said. 'Tomorrow we need to get to the train station and watch the gang. Whatever is in Left Luggage locker 3 will lead us to the criminals.'

Chapter Thirteen

'I'm going to go and check out the railway station,' Piotr said. 'Just to make sure it has a Left Luggage locker number 3.'

Andrew was blocking Piotr's way. But he didn't move when Piotr made to leave. Instead, he planted his elbows heavily on the table and dropped his chin on to his palms.

'What's the matter?' Piotr asked.

Andrew shrugged.

'Go on. What?'

Andrew raised his head slowly. 'Marcus,' he said. 'I can't believe Marcus has anything to do with a criminal gang and a hidden message and the break-in. He was so *nice* he gave us *lemonade*.'

'Even criminals have quality soft drinks,' Minnie said. 'In fact, criminals probably have nicer stuff than the rest of us. If not, what's the point of being a criminal?'

'But …' Andrew tried again, 'but he seemed so kind. Do you think maybe the letter wasn't for him at all? That the hidden message was meant to be for Omar and the post office delivered it to the wrong address? Omar had the green T-shirt, after all.'

Minnie had to admit it was odd. The fact that the T-shirt was in the dry cleaner's suggested that Omar was involved. But the letter with the hidden message had been in Marcus's tray.

'We don't know who the gang are or what they're up to,' Minnie said. 'But we'll find out at the railway station tomorrow.'

As they left the cafe, Flora twitched Minnie's sleeve. The boys went on ahead, but Minnie paused.

'It's Sylvie,' Flora said sadly. 'She still wouldn't come when you texted me.'

Minnie gave a shrug. She didn't care what Sylvie did.

'Will you at least think about making it up with her?' Flora asked.

'I'm not going to say sorry. I've got nothing to be sorry for,' Minnie said hotly.

Flora didn't reply straight away. Minnie got the impression that she was choosing her words very carefully. 'Will you just think about it?' Flora asked.

Minnie tilted her head. It wasn't a yes; it wasn't a no. It was the best Flora was going to get.

It left Minnie feeling a bit crotchety. She gave them all a short wave and went, alone, through the salon and up to the flat.

She glanced into her room. Gran wasn't there, but she had made a start on the rearranging she'd threatened – one of the beds was angled awkwardly, but at least it was possible to open the wardrobe door now.

'Minnie? Is that you?' Gran's voice came from the kitchen. Minnie went in. There was an untouched plate of biscuits on the kitchen table, a pot of tea and two empty cups. Gran hadn't poured the tea.

'Is it ready?' Minnie said, gesturing at the teapot.

'It was ready an hour ago,' Gran said. 'I expect it is cold now.'

Minnie slid into the chair opposite Gran. 'What's the matter?'

All the battleship confidence seemed to have left Gran. It was as though she'd run aground on the rocks. 'I got this ready' – Gran waved at the tea things – 'because I thought your Special Constable Wright might take me seriously. I thought he might listen. But there's been no sign of him.'

'Nothing? He hasn't even called?'

Gran looked at the cold teapot. 'I was promised a swift response. Action. But promises here seem to be as breakable as thread.'

'That's not true! Jimmy's nice!'

Gran didn't reply.

Jimmy wouldn't let them down, would he? Perhaps he was working undercover or was chasing down criminals right now. It couldn't be that he didn't care, surely? Minnie took the teapot to the sink and poured away the cold tea, splashing it up the sides and on the taps. She crammed the biscuits back in the biscuit tin.

She dropped a quick kiss on the top of Gran's head and left the room. She had to: she was way too cross to stay.

If Jimmy wasn't going to fix things, then she and the others would.

Chapter Fourteen

Gran didn't eat much that evening. Although the sizzling sound of frying vegetables and the smell of the okra alone had made Minnie's mouth water, Gran just pushed her food around her plate.

'Is everything all right?' Mum asked.

'The food is wonderful, Taiwo, really. I'm just bone-tired. I think I'll go to bed.' Gran heaved herself up and shuffled out towards the bedroom.

Mum caught Dad's eye. Dad speared a piece of food and ate it.

'Your mother,' Mum said quietly.

'What? What about her?' Dad said.

Minnie shook more salt on to her food and chewed in silence.

'Calm down. I was just going to say that I don't think your mother is settling in well.'

'She's overwhelmed, that is all,' Dad said. The tines of his fork grated across the china plate.

'Yes. I am agreeing with you, Joseph. We are in agreement.'

'Are we?'

'We are. I wonder if we can find something for her to do in the day? Perhaps a club or an activity.'

'You want her out of the house?'

'No! I want her to make friends, meet people.'

'She can help around the flat. She'd like that.'

'She's not a maid! She's our guest.'

'Guest?'

They stared at each other. Minnie had never seen Mum and Dad like this. Usually they moved and laughed together. They never snapped like dry twigs.

'You should go to bed too, Minnie,' Mum said finally.

Minnie didn't argue. She was happy to get out of there.

In the bedroom, Minnie didn't want to turn on the light. She didn't want to wake Gran. She could see the lump of Gran's body under the covers, the weird head on the window sill with Gran's wig balanced on top. The room smelled different now, of spice and flowers – Gran's body mist.

Home felt funny.

Outside felt dangerous.

And Jimmy had done nothing to help them.

Chapter Fifteen

Minnie didn't sleep well. Gran snored a little bit, but it wasn't that. It was the snappy, crotchety way that Mum and Dad had talked to each other. They were never, ever like that. As she lay in the dark staring up at the chewing-gum grey ceiling, Minnie knew the criminals were to blame. Gran didn't feel safe, so she couldn't feel comfortable. And because Gran wasn't comfortable, Mum and Dad were arguing. Well, no criminal gang was going to upset her gran and get away with it.

She had to talk to Piotr.

She got up early on Tuesday morning and dressed quietly. At the kitchen table, she swallowed her cereal almost in one gulp, rinsed the bowl and left a note for Mum and Dad.

Outside, the market traders were beginning to set up: carts rumbled into position, awnings swayed into place, goods arrived from vans and car boots. Most people had a friendly 'Morning!' for her as she walked through.

Piotr lived in the same block of flats as Andrew, at the far end of Marsh Road, beyond the market. She took the lift up to the fifth floor and rapped on his front door.

Piotr's mum answered. She was carrying his little sister, Kasia. 'Good morning, Minnie,' she said. The 'r' in the middle of 'morning' rolled like trolley wheels on cobbles in Mrs Domek's Polish accent. 'Piotr is awake, I think. Go through.'

Piotr was, but he was still in his Superman pyjamas. His room was small, but less crammed with furniture than hers, so it felt bigger. He sat on his bed. She could see the comic he'd been reading tucked beneath the duvet like a teddy.

'What's up?' he asked.

'Mum and Dad,' she said simply. 'We have to find out what's going on to save Mum and Dad.'

'What do you mean?'

'They're sniping at each other worse than me and Andrew. Worse than me and Sylvie!'

Piotr recoiled. 'That's bad. What do you need us to do?'

'Did you get to the railway station yesterday? Was there a Left Luggage place? Are we on the right track?'

'Yes, yes and I think so.'

'Good. I think my family are depending on it.'

The railway station was at the top of the town. The tracks climbed up over arches, then ran behind the main shopping street until they reached the platforms of the old sandstone building. Trains shuttled past regularly, pushing through the air on their clattering journeys.

At 2.30 p.m., Flora was already there, waiting at the passenger drop-off point outside the main doors. She was wearing a pale lemon top with pale brown trousers. Minnie thought they might even be slacks. They made Minnie's jeans from the market look tatty. She scowled and let Piotr and Andrew say the hellos.

'No Sylvie today?' Piotr asked.

Flora flushed a little, but just shook her head.

Minnie felt a prickle of discomfort. Guilt? No. She squished the thought immediately.

'Any sign of Omar? Or Marcus?' Piotr asked.

'Omar, I expect,' Andrew said hopefully, not ready to admit Marcus was up to no good.

'Neither so far,' Flora replied. 'Lots of people in business suits and trainers queuing for coffee, but that's about it.'

There were lots of people at the station – women on phones, men carrying briefcases, all ignoring each other, like ants in an anthill.

'Left Luggage is inside,' Piotr said.

The station was big, with six platforms beyond the ticket barrier. The main concourse was breezy, with a glass ceiling high above their heads and pigeons patrolling the area, searching out unauthorised crisps and pecking them into submission.

The ticket office was on one side, along with a tourist information booth. The other side of the concourse had coffee bars and news-stands and was more crowded.

'This way,' Piotr said. He led them away from the bustle of people staring up at departure boards. They passed the ticket office and information booth, and with the main concourse behind them they were getting closer to a smaller, side entrance to the station. Black tape had been stuck to the tiled floor to show the way out. Their footsteps echoed on the white tiles and the sound bounced back off the glass roof. There were fewer people in this part of the station.

The Left Luggage office was just before the side entrance.

'I want to see locker 3,' Minnie said to Piotr.

She could still just about make out the departures board, black panels with the destinations glowing orange. The time, like a retro digital watch, ticked above the town names: 14:38.

'Let's take a look,' Piotr said. 'But we have to be quick. Whoever the hidden message was for, they'll be here any minute.'

Andrew and Flora stood on guard outside, while Piotr and Minnie went in. Left Luggage was a small room lined with lockers, a bit like a leisure centre changing room but without the smell of sweat and socks. Some lockers had keys hanging in the doors, others were shut with the keys missing. They were all a shade of beige; the walls were beige too. It wasn't a room anyone would want to spend time in. Each locker was numbered. Minnie found locker number 3. It was locked tight, with the key missing. She rattled the door, but it didn't open.

Whatever was inside was important enough to commit a break-in for, to use a child messenger, to frighten Gran and set her parents fighting.

She had to know what was worth all that.

'We need to find somewhere to keep watch,' Minnie said.

Back outside, Andrew was facing the distant concourse; Flora was facing the side entrance. They both turned as Minnie and Piotr joined them. 'No sign of Omar yet,' Andrew said.

'Nor of Marcus,' Flora added.

'We'll stake out the Left Luggage,' Minnie said, 'but we can't just stand here in a big group, we're really noticeable.' They were the only group at the station without a harassed-looking adult counting heads.

'Trainspotting,' Flora said.

'What?' Andrew wasn't the only one who was confused.

'Trainspotting. I brought us all a notebook and pencil. If anyone asks, we're looking out for a rare engine that's due to pass through later today. We can split up and keep an eye out for Omar or Marcus. One of us should stay near the Left Luggage at all times.'

'Great,' Andrew said, taking his notebook. 'I love trains. If I wasn't going to be a global superstar when I grow up, I'd be a train driver.'

Minnie and Piotr took theirs too.

'Trainspotters usually stand at the ends of platforms,' Flora said, 'but anywhere you can see the tracks is good. Andrew, come with me, we'll watch the main entrance to the station.'

Flora and Andrew set off towards the open concourse with their notebooks open.

Minnie wanted to stay close to Left Luggage. A section of the walkway had been fenced off by a cordon of orange plastic barriers, there was some kind of maintenance work going on. It caught her attention. It was far enough from the Left Luggage office that anyone visiting the lockers might not notice it, but close enough that it still had a clear view of the door. She crept closer to the barriers and a big Health and Safety notice: NO HARD HAT, NO JOB. No workers around. Good. No one looking in their direction. Perfect. Minnie vaulted the barrier, crouched behind the big sign and shuffled up to let Piotr in too.

They waited.

The clock flashed the minutes. Time seemed to slow right down. Minnie was getting cramp in her leg from being so hunched up.

They watched the side entrance for Marcus, for Omar. Which one of them was at the heart of this?

Then Piotr gasped. Minnie felt him freeze beside her. She realised why.

Two people sauntered through the side entrance. Two people were approaching Left Luggage.

Minnie didn't dare move a muscle. Hardly dared breathe.

Omar and Marcus might see.

They were both here, walking side by side.

They were both criminals.

Chapter Sixteen

'They're working together,' Minnie whispered once the two men had gone inside.

'But to do what?' Piotr replied.

'There's only one way to find out.' Minnie crept out from behind the barrier and scurried across the tiled floor. Piotr followed. They both pressed their backs to the outside wall of the Left Luggage office and crouched down. Minnie risked leaning to her right so that she could peek around the door frame. She felt Piotr ducking to see through the crook of her arm.

Inside, Omar and Marcus stood before locker 3. Omar ran his hand along the top of the bank of lockers. His fingers clasped something. He took it down. A key! Minnie covered her mouth to stop a groan. The key had been left inside the room. If only they'd looked they might have found it! She cursed the fact that it was too late now.

Omar slid the key into locker number 3 and opened the door with a squeak of rusty hinges.

Minnie held her breath as Marcus reached inside. He lifted out an object carefully. It was the size of a football, round, wrapped in a loose cloth cover.

He flipped the cloth aside.

Minnie caught a glance.

She saw a brown nose. A copper cheek. A bronze eye. A drape of metal beads picked out in red and orange across the smooth plane of a forehead.

She bit her lip. Marcus was holding a head.

He flipped the cloth back and turned to Omar, who was leaning in close and breathing hard. 'Don't watch the merchandise, watch the door!' Marcus complained. 'You're here as hired muscle, not as an art critic.'

'You say I am hired, but you are very bad at paying my bills,' Omar replied. He stepped back with a sullen grunt.

Minnie pulled away from the door and hustled Piotr to move, move, move.

He broke into a run.

They both raced towards the busiest part of the concourse, ducking under a window cleaner's ladder, dodging around groups of families watching the departures flicker and flutter.

Minnie glanced back. Omar stood outside Left Luggage like a bouncer outside a nightclub. He hadn't seen them. They had better keep it that way. Minnie pulled Piotr inside a newsagent. A bank of chocolates and newspapers stacked in a plastic holder hid them from sight.

'A head!' Minnie whispered. 'A head in a storage locker! What's going on, Piotr?'

'Did you hear what he said? He called it merchandise. Art.'

Minnie felt her cheeks redden. Of course it wasn't a real head; it was a sculpture. She knew that. But it had still shocked her; it had looked so lifelike. She didn't have time to answer though. Flora and Andrew dashed into the shop.

'We saw you run,' Flora said. 'Are you all right?'

'Oi!' the person behind the counter said. 'No more than two unaccompanied schoolchildren in the shop. Two of you, hop it.'

'It's all right,' Piotr said. 'We're all going.'

He checked the concourse before leading them out of the shop – no sign of Marcus or Omar. They tried to blend in with the crowd, while also watching for the criminals. But there was no sign of either man. They must have taken their prize and left in a hurry.

'So,' Flora said. 'What did you see?'

Minnie described it quickly – the metal eyes, nose, cheek. It still gave her the shivers, but it was better to be able to say it was made of bronze and not someone's body parts.

Flora pulled out her phone and tapped quickly. 'I'm just searching "bronze" and "Nigeria" to see what comes up,' she explained.

They were walking out of the station and across the car park towards the footpath that was a shortcut back to Marsh Road, when Flora whistled. There was nowhere to stop, so Minnie had to crane her neck to see what she was looking at.

On the screen were tens of photos, all showing different bronze heads.

'It must have been a bust,' Flora said.

Andrew sniggered.

'Not that sort of bust,' Flora said. 'It means a sculpture of a head,' she explained.

'Then why's it called a bust?' Piotr said, laughing.

'I don't know.' Flora blushed.

'And it was Marcus and Omar?' Andrew asked. 'Not just Omar? That's so unfair. I liked Marcus.'

'I wonder,' said Piotr. 'I wonder if Marcus gets

Omar to do his dirty work for him? I wonder if Marcus was lookout in the alley when Omar burgled your flat?'

'Like a minion?' Andrew said. 'Oh, I've always wanted a minion.'

They had reached the footpath and dropped down off the road. They had to walk in single file past the overgrown buddleia bushes and the archway lock-ups.

Once they hit the open space in front of the arches, they spread out again.

Minnie could still picture the bust – she couldn't help smiling at the word too – cradled in the cloth in Marcus's hands. Its nose and lips, so haughty and proud. The swathe of beads across its forehead.

She gasped. 'A crown! It was wearing a crown!' Something Gran had said came back to her. Stories tumbled around in her mind in a whirl of words and images. 'The kings of Ife wear beaded crowns. That was the head of a king!'

Flora tapped her phone again. The pictures changed. This time all the bronze heads wore crowns, just like Gran had described.

'There was something else,' Minnie said. 'Gran said that the king of Ife had nightmares that his ancestors were angry. He shut down an archaeological site where they were digging up the heads of the ancestors.'

'What if someone didn't listen to the king?' Flora said. 'What if someone has been digging up the bronze heads anyway? They'd have to do it in secret, without anyone finding out. They'd have to smuggle them out of the country and use hidden messages and ciphers to avoid being caught.'

'But they're just plain metal heads,' Andrew said. 'They're not made of gold. They're not covered in jewels. Are they really worth going to all that trouble for?'

Flora tapped once more at her phone. No one spoke. In the distance, they could hear the rattling roll of a train pulling into the station.

Then Flora said, 'They've got one head in the British Museum; there are a few others, not many, in other museums around the world. But an Ife head hasn't been sold at auction since the 1980s ... and when it did,' she said slowly, 'it went for more than a million pounds.'

Chapter Seventeen

They walked back to Marsh Road in a stunned silence. A million pounds! Last century! What would it be worth now? Two million? Ten million? More?

Except that however much it was, Minnie didn't think it was worth scaring Gran for. Or using young boys as messengers. Or disturbing the dreams of a king. The bronze heads had been buried with their owners hundreds of years ago. They shouldn't have been touched at all.

Until a few days ago, Minnie had never heard of Ife. But now she felt as though her life had become tangled up in a web going back centuries and crossing continents. She remembered how her Nigerian cousins had laughed at her for sounding funny, for eating weird food like chicken nuggets, for not knowing how to light a lantern when a power cut happened.

She'd felt left out.

But now a part of Nigeria – the bronzes, the boy, even Gran – had come to her and needed her help.

'Are you OK?' Flora asked quietly. She'd fallen in step with Minnie, a little way ahead of the boys.

'I'm just a bit upset, I suppose,' Minnie said. She had no idea how to begin to tell Flora what she was feeling.

'Sometimes,' said Flora, 'when I feel upset, I like to imagine that I'm just a dream that someone is having. That I'm not real.'

'You can be a bit odd sometimes,' Minnie replied.

'Sylvie says that too,' Flora agreed, 'but I don't mind. What's making you upset?'

Would Flora understand? She didn't know what it was like to have two different ways to be – to be British and Nigerian at once – and how the two didn't always work so well together.

She was a twin though. So maybe she did know something about being two different people at the same time. But Minnie didn't want to talk about Sylvie, or the fact that she wasn't there with them. She didn't want to have to explain herself to anyone. She shrugged.

Flora dropped back to talk to Piotr. The moment for sharing was gone.

'I think we should call the police,' Piotr said.

'Can we call Jimmy?' Flora said eagerly.

Jimmy. Minnie felt a surge of anger at the mention of his name. Gran had sat with her pot of tea turning stone cold waiting for his call.

He hadn't rung. He didn't care.

'There's no point calling the police,' Minnie said. 'They won't do anything.'

'But we have to,' Flora said. 'We can't stop a smuggling gang on our own. And it isn't just the illegal art, is it? Or have you forgotten about the boy?'

It was worse remembering the boy. What if he was in danger? In trouble? And Jimmy hadn't done a single thing to stop it. It was all Jimmy's fault if the boy ended up hurt.

'Fine,' she snapped at Flora. 'Call your precious Jimmy. But don't be surprised if nothing happens.'

Minnie stalked ahead of the others. She let her long legs carry her forward, like a missile set on a target. She just wanted to get home.

She could hear Flora's voice speaking into her phone. 'Yes, yes, that would be good. Yes, we'll meet you there.' Then running. She glanced back. Flora was running to catch her up.

Flora smiled, her milk white cheeks peached from the

effort. 'I just spoke to Jimmy,' she said. 'He says he'll meet us in the cafe in ten minutes.'

Minnie was stunned. Jimmy was going to drop everything for Flora, when he hadn't done a single thing for her family even though it had been days since the break-in. She glared at her friend as though she wanted to hit her. Which she did.

Minnie walked in stony silence to the cafe. Inside, she didn't reply to Eileen's cheery 'Good afternoon!' She sat in a booth and stared out of the window.

The others piled in too, chatting about the bronze head, the millions, having minions and what Jimmy would say about it all.

Minnie didn't join in. Didn't say a word.

She was too angry.

Chapter Eighteen

Jimmy, as he'd promised Flora, was at the cafe inside ten minutes. He was in uniform, neat and polished as always. He smoothed down his mousy hair, which had a tiny trace of hat-head. Then he squeezed into the bench beside Andrew.

'So,' he asked, 'what's the big emergency?'

He was joking about it!

Minnie refused to look him in the eye. She tugged a napkin from its holder and began to tear it up, making a mouse-nest pile on the tabletop.

Eileen put a frothy coffee down in front of Jimmy.

'We saw a smuggled bronze,' Flora said. 'We've been on their trail for a few days, but today we saw them at the drop.'

'The drop?' Jimmy asked.

'It's a pre-arranged place where criminals pass goods to one another,' Flora explained.

Jimmy chuckled. 'Yes, I know what a drop is. What I'm wondering is what you lot have been up to now.'

Minnie watched the bustle of the market, the apples, strawberries, potatoes, being twisted into paper bags by the traders. She couldn't look at Jimmy.

Flora was waiting for her to speak, to explain about the break-in, the cipher, the missing boy and the head of the king. But she wasn't going to tell him anything. If he'd wanted to know, he'd had days to get in touch. Minnie rolled her shredded napkin into balls.

Piotr gave her a funny look, then he turned to Jimmy. 'We found a cipher and a hidden message that led us to the railway station, where we saw Marcus Mainwaring from the gallery and Omar from the dry cleaner's take a bronze head from a locker. If we're right, the head is worth millions.'

'*If* you're right,' Jimmy said. 'You'd better show me this cipher, and the hidden message.'

Flora riffled through her trusty backpack and pulled out her copies of the postcard and the letter from the school. She handed them to Jimmy and showed him how the secret message was revealed that led them to the locker. 'Minnie took the photographs and I turned the photos into replicas,' she said proudly.

'So these aren't the originals? Where did you find the originals?'

He was asking Minnie. She didn't reply.

'Well,' Jimmy said, examining them, 'they're peculiar, I'll give you that. But if you made these they probably don't count as evidence.'

Flora looked dismayed. 'But I had to make them. How else would we have read the message?'

'I understand, but they've been manipulated on a computer. And, in general, manipulation isn't good for evidence.'

'What would be good evidence?' Andrew demanded.

Jimmy took a sip of his drink, then wiped the froth from his top lip. 'Listen, I don't have much to go on. There might not even be a case here. What I'll do is I'll talk to Marcus, just an informal chat. I might be able to uncover something that means I could get a warrant. But there's not a lot to link him to a crime.'

Minnie felt her teeth grind together. Not a lot to link Marcus to a crime? What about the break-in? Wasn't that a crime? And the peanut boy? Wasn't he worth rescuing? Jimmy hadn't even mentioned that, and the police file had been sent to him personally.

'Can we come too?' Flora asked.

'What, all of you?' Jimmy chuckled. 'No. I can't take junior detectives with me, even on routine enquiries. You can wait here.'

Minnie finally spoke. 'No way,' she said.

Chapter Nineteen

'I am not waiting here,' Minnie said.

Jimmy looked startled.

'We've done all the investigating. It isn't fair for you to take over now and keep us out.'

'Minnie,' Piotr warned in a low voice.

'No,' Minnie said. 'It's true. It isn't fair.'

Jimmy held up his hands. 'Minnie, wait. Listen, if you feel that strongly about it, maybe we can work something out. But I really can't go and interview a suspect with four children in tow. No matter how talented those children are,' he said.

'Not four, just me,' Minnie said. 'I'm coming with you.'

'Yes,' Andrew said. 'You could take Minnie with you. She's so tall, Marcus might think she's your work experience or something.'

'Wait,' Flora said suddenly. 'You can't. Marcus has met you before. You've been in his gallery already. He won't talk if he recognises you.'

Minnie paused. She hated to admit that Flora was right, but it was true.

'Fine,' she said. 'But he hasn't met Piotr, has he? Piotr can go instead of me.'

She glared at Piotr. She knew it wasn't fair to be cross with him, but she couldn't help herself.

'I'll take Piotr,' Jimmy said. 'But remember, I'm in charge. We're just having an informal chat, not leading the charge of the light brigade.'

'What?' Andrew asked.

'We're not attacking the Death Star,' Jimmy said with a smile.

'Right.'

'Come on, let's go and see this Marcus chap.'

Chapter Twenty

Minnie didn't really want to wait with the others while Piotr was away doing the investigating. But she had no choice. The flat was miserable with Gran still hurt and upset. The salon was crotchety; Mum was edgy. She had nowhere else to go.

She sat in silence, staring out of the window.

'You know,' Flora said softly, 'sometimes you and Sylvie can be very similar.'

Minnie didn't reply. She turned her back and watched the street.

Flora was wrong. She was nothing like Sylvie.

Chapter Twenty-One

Piotr followed Jimmy out of the cafe. He glanced back. Minnie's face was obscured by low sunlight reflecting on the window, so he couldn't tell what she was thinking. But he could imagine. Jimmy whistled as he walked through the market, nodding hello at some of the traders, and even some of the shoppers. Just like the Jimmy who had been so kind to Piotr when his dad had been in trouble. It didn't make sense.

'Ikonik, right?' Jimmy asked.

Piotr nodded.

'I've always meant to go in there but never got around to it.'

Piotr shrugged.

'I'm not much of an art fan, but my girlfriend likes that kind of thing.'

Jimmy glanced down at Piotr. He frowned. Then he stopped walking. 'Listen. Is there something going on that I'm not getting? Minnie hardly spoke to me, and now you're giving me the silent treatment. I'm helping to find this strange bit of art, aren't I? Isn't that what you want?'

Piotr couldn't help feeling that, for a police officer, Jimmy could be a bit dense sometimes. 'I expect it's because of the break-in and the missing boy and how you haven't been bothered about any of it,' Piotr said, his voice exasperated.

'Break-in?' Jimmy's voice rose an octave.

'Yes. The break-in at Minnie's flat when the boy's suitcase was stolen. You know.'

'I certainly do not know.'

Piotr shoved his hands deep in his pockets. He felt as though he were being told off, but that wasn't fair, because it was Jimmy who hadn't done what he was supposed to.

'Sorry, Piotr, sorry. I didn't mean to snap. I was just surprised, that's all.'

Surprised? Piotr looked up. Jimmy's face looked confused, his forehead creased, his eyes wrinkled at the corners. But he didn't look guilty. He tried to remember exactly what Flora had said to Jimmy in the cafe. Had she mentioned the break-in? No. She'd just told Jimmy about the cipher and the Left Luggage – that's what they'd all been focused on.

'Don't you have a file on your desk,' Piotr asked, 'that reports a break-in at Minnie's flat on Sunday morning? The only thing stolen was a suitcase of boys' clothes that Minnie's gran had accidentally taken from the airport. The cipher was inside that suitcase. That's how we know it's all linked.'

'There are a lot of files on my desk,' Jimmy said softly. 'A whole heap got dumped on me. I haven't had time to look through. I didn't realise, I promise. I didn't know.'

The sounds of the market seemed to fade as Piotr watched the emotions flash across Jimmy's face: sadness, embarrassment, then determination. 'I'll go and see Minnie's gran right now. If there's a missing boy, child services will have to get involved. There's no time to waste. I'd better apologise to Minnie too.'

Jimmy turned on his heel, ready to weave his way back through the fruit and veg stall, the frying onions, the shouts of the traders, to head back to the cafe.

Piotr grabbed his arm. He could barely get his fingers around the solid muscle, but the touch was enough to halt Jimmy. 'I think the only apology Minnie would accept,' Piotr said, 'is if you investigate Marcus right now. It's only been an hour since he was at the station. That's exactly the right time to ask him questions about it. It's what Minnie wants you to do.'

Jimmy glanced back at the cafe, then at the road ahead. He gave a firm nod. 'You're right. Let's see what we can find out.'

Ikonik was open. Piotr was pleased to see Marcus standing inside, with two customers. He hadn't gone to ground after the drop. But was the Ife head here at the gallery?

Jimmy pushed open the door and stepped inside. Piotr followed.

Marcus smiled, perhaps a little nervously, as he saw Jimmy and his uniform. 'One small moment,' they heard him say to his customers. 'Do please yodel should you need any assistance.'

Then he approached Jimmy and Piotr, and his voice dropped discreetly.

'Hello, officer, how can I be of service?'

'I'm not here in any official capacity,' Jimmy said in a friendly voice. 'More idle curiosity. You're on my patch so I thought my young friend and I might just say hello. I'm SPC Wright. The art here is African, is it?'

'African, Oriental and Australian,' Marcus corrected him. 'We have a very broad range of interests.'

Jimmy browsed the objects on the wall, the gold cloth, the water bottles, before heading towards the counter. Marcus hovered around him, like a moth by a lamp. The wire tray was still on the counter. Jimmy rested an elbow on the top and glanced at the envelopes. His friendly grin didn't waiver.

'Is it difficult to source?' Jimmy asked.

Marcus laughed. 'Oh, not at all. Artists are very keen to be able to exhibit. We always have more artists than we could possibly show. We're very lucky.'

'We?' Jimmy asked.

'I have silent partners,' Marcus explained. 'While I'm delighted to make your acquaintance, I'm afraid that the uniform is a little disconcerting. Perhaps I could ask you to come back on your day off and I'll give you a proper tour?'

Jimmy nodded warmly. 'Yes, of course, I understand.' He pushed himself upright.

Was that it? Piotr was about to break his promise about no attacks on the Death Star and ask Marcus about the bronze head and the peanut boy, when Jimmy turned.

'Just one more thing,' he said. 'Is this all of your stock? Everything you have for sale?'

Piotr saw something flash across Marcus's face. Irritation? Fear? Then the smooth, poised gallery owner was back. 'Do see for yourself. Come.' He headed into the back of the shop. Jimmy gave Piotr a curt nod and they followed behind.

There was a tiny, cramped kitchen just off the corridor – a sink, a cupboard, a microwave. Beyond that was a white door. Marcus opened the door to reveal a compact bathroom: a toilet and another mini sink. There was a paperback book balanced on the edge of it.

'This is my whole operation,' Marcus said, spreading his hands to include the sink. 'Everything I have to sell is on display. Why would it not be? I need to sell it to make money.'

Jimmy smiled warmly. 'Of course. I was just hoping we might get a sneak preview of your newest art.'

'You can. In the gallery.'

'Well, we'd best be off,' Jimmy said. 'But you can be sure I'll be back.'

'I look forward to it,' Marcus replied.

Out on the street, Piotr shook his head. 'Minnie isn't going to like this. You didn't ask him about the railway station. Or the head. Or the break-in.'

'Hush, not outside the shop.' Jimmy walked purpose-fully away from the entrance.

Piotr followed. 'Jimmy!'

'I'm thinking,' Jimmy said.

Piotr waited five seconds. 'Well?'

'Still thinking.'

They were at the market before Jimmy spoke again. 'I got a weird feeling from him. Not a pleasant one. And there was a letter with a Nigerian stamp in his tray, just like Flora said. But I can't get at it without a warrant. I think I need to take this case right back to the beginning, dig out the file on my desk and start treating this as a full enquiry. I'll start by getting the scene of crime officers around to Minnie's flat.'

'They won't find anything. It was days ago now.' Piotr was beginning to feel frustrated. No wonder Minnie had been cross.

'Maybe, but this needs to be done by the book. If you're right, then I'll come to the same conclusions, but this time with hard evidence.'

'You mean you'll get to where we are now, but in a week's time when it's too late?'

'I'll make sure it's done quickly. I'll find a reason to get that warrant, especially when my superiors learn that there is a young boy whose whereabouts are unknown. The crime scene team will be there before you know it. Don't worry, Piotr, I've got this. Tell Minnie I'll be in touch soon.'

Piotr shook his head. 'I think she's heard that before.'

'I mean it this time,' Jimmy promised.

Chapter Twenty-Two

Piotr trudged back to the cafe, where the others were waiting for him. His hands were stuffed deep into his pockets, his shoulders scrunched towards his ears. Jimmy had been horribly polite to Marcus. The crime scene team, who should have been sent on Sunday, were only now being dispatched. His news was going to go down like an elephant in a lift shaft. He pushed the door open with his elbow.

'Piotr!' Andrew said, shuffling up on his bench. 'How did it go? Did you find the bronze? Or the boy? Will we get a share in the million pounds?'

'No, no, and why on earth would we?' Piotr said. He sank down heavily.

Minnie was watching him. Her face was pinched, wary. He wasn't going to enjoy telling her any of this.

'Well?' Minnie said.

Piotr sighed. 'Jimmy didn't know about the break-in. He says he's got a huge pile of work on his desk and he hasn't got around to it yet.'

Minnie clicked her tongue against her teeth. 'Seems to me that Gran's right. She thinks it's worse than Lagos. People with money get results, people without it don't.' Her eyes flashed towards Flora as she spoke.

'That's not true,' Piotr said. 'Jimmy says he's sending the fingerprint people to your flat now.'

'And what good will that do? Dad changed the locks and Gran's been cleaning. They won't find a thing. And Lowdog definitely won't tell the police who he saw in the alleyway that day.'

'He wants to investigate properly,' Piotr tried again.

'He's had his chance,' Minnie said. 'This is down to us. It's always been down to us.'

Andrew looked sheepish. 'It's getting a bit late, Minnie. Mum needs me to get dinner. Cheese and tomato sandwiches. I hate tomato, but Mum says I need to be braver about pips, so I agreed to try.'

Minnie managed a weak smile.

Flora stood up. 'I'd better get back too. What should I say to Sylvie?'

Minnie slumped lower in her seat. It was fine for Flora

and Sylvie. They got whatever they wanted at the drop of a hat – Jimmy had come running when Flora called him.

The twins had everything. Except … Minnie looked at Andrew who was trying to cheer her up. And Piotr, solid and patient by her side. Sylvie didn't have them. Didn't have friends like them. The whole reason the row with Sylvie had happened was because Sylvie had wanted to feel a part of the gang.

Minnie bit her lip.

Andrew and Flora headed out of the door with a wave goodbye.

It was just Minnie and Piotr left. 'Are you all right?' he asked.

'I don't want to give up,' she replied quietly, 'but I don't know what to do.'

'Yes. I thought Jimmy would come and find the boy and the thieves and fix it all for us.'

'Me too.'

'I guess grown-ups don't always come to the rescue,' Piotr said sadly.

'That poor boy,' Minnie said. 'His fingers and toes might be safe, but the gang put him on the flight all by himself. Gran said he was little, much younger than we are. Can you imagine being at an airport all alone? The plane taking off? The gates and carousels and all the crowds and people at the other end? Where is he? Where are his family? How has he ended up with thieves and grave robbers?'

'Like Oliver Twist,' Piotr said. 'I saw the film once. With the singing. Oliver ends up with a gang of pick-pockets and he doesn't know how to get out.'

'We need to find him, Piotr.'

'How do we do that?'

'That's just it. I have no idea.'

Chapter Twenty-Three

'Marcus or Omar know where he is,' Minnie said. 'They used the cipher, they took his T-shirt to be cleaned. One of them did, anyway. They could tell us.'

'You can't confront them,' Piotr said. 'It would be too dangerous. And you've got no proof. Remember what Jimmy said about needing evidence?'

Minnie waved the objection away. Jimmy had been talking about evidence in court, not evidence to help find a missing boy.

Though Piotr was right, the two men probably were dangerous. If she went alone.

'You'll come with me, won't you?' Minnie asked. 'They'll be closing their shops soon, going home. We could follow them, find out where they live. Peanut boy might be there.' Outside, the market was winding down for the day, stalls packed into cardboard boxes and car boots.

'How can we follow two people and stay together?' Piotr pointed out.

'We can't do nothing!' Minnie insisted. The few customers still in the cafe before closing turned to look at her. She hadn't meant to shout. She pressed her fingers to her temples. 'I'm sorry, I just want to do something.'

'We will.' Piotr ducked his head so that he was looking her right in the eye. 'But not on our own. We need to wait for the others too.'

'We could follow one of them then. Tonight, just the two of us?'

Piotr sighed. 'Fine. Fine. I know when I'm beaten.'

'Thank you!' Minnie hated feeling helpless. It was the worst thing ever. With something to do, the world already seemed better. She stood up and pulled on her jacket.

'Right now?' Piotr asked.

'Right now,' Minnie said.

She led the way down Marsh Road towards the theatre. She crossed the street and ducked behind a plane tree. From there, they could see the row of single-storey shops – Ikonik and Ahmed's Cleaning Experts included.

The gallery was already closed. Heavy steel bars had come down over the glass; the front door was shuttered too. They had missed Marcus.

But the 'OPEN' sign still hung in the door of the dry cleaner's. They could follow Omar.

They waited.

'What time does the shop close?' Piotr whispered.

'Hush,' Minnie replied. She had no idea. She hoped it wasn't too late; she was getting pins and needles in her foot from crouching behind the tree.

It wasn't too long.

After about fifteen minutes of waiting, Omar came out of the shop. He whistled to himself as he locked the front door and pocketed the keys.

'Watch him!' Minnie said. She was getting ready to dash from their tree to the next one, to follow him all the way home, when –

Omar pulled a different set of keys out of his pocket and waved them towards a white van parked near the curb. The van beeped twice and its orange hazard lights blinked on and off.

Omar was driving home.

'He'll get away!' Minnie said.

Omar pulled open the door and disappeared from view inside. The engine started and he pulled out into the busy evening traffic.

Minnie stepped out from behind the tree. She dodged

the line of cars and ran to the other side of the street. She ran for a while: the van was still in view, caught at a set of lights. Her arms pumped at her sides; she willed her legs to move even faster.

She might catch up.

She might.

The lights changed and the van pulled away. Omar turned a corner and, by the time Minnie reached it, he was gone.

Minnie slowed down. She stopped running. She stood with her hands on her knees, her head down, trying to catch her breath. She'd lost him.

She stood slowly and walked back towards Piotr. He hadn't even run. He'd stayed outside the dry cleaner's. She felt a hot wave of anger and her eyes stung – sweat or tears? She wiped them crossly with the back of her sleeve. In front of the shop now, she scowled at Piotr.

'You didn't even chase him!'

'Minnie,' he said, 'there was no way we could keep up with a van.'

'We might have!'

'Stop shouting.'

'You stop shouting!'

Piotr frowned at her. 'You're being stupid.'

What? What was he talking about? 'No, I'm not.'

'Yes. You are. You've been so angry and cross with everybody that you won't even listen. You've been mean to Flora, and Jimmy. And now me. And Sylvie has been avoiding us because you set her up.'

'I didn't!'

'Yes, you did. You know Derek. He was bound to be horrible to her. And you made her go by herself anyway.'

Minnie could have screamed and stamped her feet and yelled at the darkening sky.

Because she knew Piotr was right.

'I don't have to listen to you!' she shouted as loud as she could. Then she ran.

She ran away from him and didn't once look back.

Chapter Twenty-Four

When Minnie arrived at the salon, she had a stitch in her side and her eyes were brimming with hot, angry tears. She let herself in and was surprised to hear shuffling and muttering coming from the back hallway. A second break-in?

She crept slowly through the dark salon; the black chairs were lumpy crouching shapes in the gloom. There was a light on near the back door.

A police officer. And Mum. They stood together looking at the lock Dad had replaced. The police officer was a blonde woman with a black briefcase. She had a uniform, but it was less bulky than Jimmy's. Minnie realised the woman was wearing an Aertex shirt, rather than the protective vest that Jimmy wore. The shirt had 'SOCO' printed on the back in yellow.

Scene of crime officer.

Finally.

Though, by the look on the woman's face, she was too late anyway. 'I haven't been able to lift any usable prints,' she was saying to Mum. 'I'm sorry. The back door is clean and the bedroom is too.'

'Of course it's clean,' Minnie muttered. 'You're days too late.'

'Please ignore my daughter,' Mum said firmly. 'People who are frightened can often seem rude. But then people who are rude seem rude as well. It can be hard to tell the difference.'

Why was everyone out to get her? Minnie stomped away from the two of them. She'd had enough of everyone today.

But even her bedroom wasn't safe. Gran was sitting on her bed, reading.

Grr.

Minnie kicked off her trainers and threw herself on to her bed. She twisted the duvet until it was completely covering her. All she could see was the narrow canyon of world between the dark mattress and the shadowy duvet sky.

'Bad day?' Gran asked mildly.

Minnie made a noise that said, 'Leave me alone!'

'Friends or family?'

Gran wasn't leaving her alone. Minnie tugged down the duvet a tiny, tiny bit until she could peep out and see Gran. She hadn't moved, but her book had dropped into her lap and she was smiling at Minnie as though she could fix whatever it was that was wrong.

'What?' Minnie snapped.

'Friends or family? It's only people we really care about who can upset us like this. Stones thrown by strangers have no effect, but stones thrown by friends sting. Don't you think?'

'Is that from your book?' Minnie asked crossly.

Gran laughed. 'No. I made it up myself. I am hoping to see it printed on a tea towel and sell millions of copies so that we will be rich.'

Minnie pulled the cover down a little further. Now her whole head was sticking out. The rest of her body felt hot and weighed down. She kicked to get some air in.

'Why don't you tell me what went wrong, eh?'

Minnie sighed. 'I had a row with Piotr. Because I had a row with Sylvie.'

Gran said nothing. She waited.

'I was a tiny bit mean, I suppose,' Minnie said. 'But she deserved it. And Piotr shouldn't take her side.'

Gran still said nothing.

'And if she were nicer, then Derek might have been nicer. So it's her fault really.'

Gran closed her book and set it on the window sill. 'What will you do now that you are right but on your own?'

Was she right though? Somehow, Minnie knew that she wasn't entirely one-hundred-per-cent right. She didn't reply.

'Sorry goes a long way, you know,' Gran said. 'Even the great tricksters in stories know that. We need our friends more than we need our pride.'

Gran stood up then with a puffing heave. She walked to the door. 'You sleep on it,' she said. 'I'm going to speak with your mother. We never did sort out the egg business.'

Chapter Twenty-Five

The following morning, Minnie went into the bathroom to get some privacy before taking out her phone.

She dialled Sylvie's number.

It rang.

Her thumb hovered over the 'end call' button. But she forced herself to let it ring.

A sleepy voice answered. 'Hello?'

'Sylvie? It's Minnie. I'm calling to say sorry. That you had to investigate on your own. That Derek was rude to you. There. I've said it. That's all.'

There was a long pause. Minnie could hear Sylvie breathe gently. Her grip tightened on the phone.

'Apology accepted,' Sylvie said finally.

'Good. Right. Bye, then.'

'Wait!' Sylvie said. 'Are you investigating anything today? What's going on? Where are you in the case?'

Minnie had no idea where they were in the case. Nowhere. 'Dunno,' she said.

'Oh. Fine. Well, I can't help today anyway. I've got performance classes. And I'm probably meeting my dad or something later. So, even if you needed me, I couldn't come. I'll see you around.' Sylvie sounded crotchety and weird again.

Minnie sighed. This apology business was more complicated than she'd thought.

When Sylvie was off the phone, Minnie called Piotr's flat. It was a bit early for Piotr, who liked to sleep in, but he had a younger sister, who was practically still a baby, so the Domeks were usually awake with the dawn.

His mum answered and got Piotr to the phone.

'I apologised to Sylvie,' Minnie said, before he even had a chance to say hello.

'You didn't?' He sounded shocked. 'I never, ever thought you would. What did she say?'

'Something about a class. I don't know. So, listen, can we be friends again?'

'We were never not friends. I'm sorry I shouted at you,' Piotr said.

'I think I might have shouted first,' Minnie admitted.

Piotr laughed. Minnie did too. It felt like all the tension of the last few days lifted with that laugh. As though she'd been carrying a heavy suitcase and now she'd been allowed to put it down.

'Listen,' Piotr said. 'I didn't get a chance to tell you last night, but I didn't run after the van because when I looked through the dry cleaner's window I noticed something.'

'What?' Minnie pressed the phone closer to her ear.

'The T-shirt was still hanging in the shop. And it had something pinned to it. A label or something. I couldn't make it out because it was too dark. We need to take a closer look at the T-shirt.'

Just then there was a bang on the bathroom door.

'Minnie?' Dad's voice. 'What are you doing in there? There's a queue out here!'

'Huh.' Mum's voice. 'I knew one bathroom wasn't enough for the four of us.'

Dad again. 'It's fine if people don't hog it.'

'We have to go back to the dry cleaner's then,' Minnie said to Piotr.

'We've been there a lot,' he replied worriedly. 'He might get suspicious.'

'Flora hasn't been.'

'Yes, you're right. She and Sylvie can investigate this time.'

'Sylvie has a class,' Minnie said pointedly.

Piotr chuckled. 'Don't start.'

'Minnie!' The bangs on the bathroom door were solid thumps now.

'Coming!' she yelled. 'Call Flora, Piotr. I'll meet you there.'

Minnie was the first to arrive at the bench opposite ACE. What if today was the day Omar finally cleaned the T-shirt? What if he took it back to the peanut boy before Flora got there? Should Minnie follow? Should she go on her own? She forced herself to sit. Her trainers scuffed the dust beneath the bench. The sun was warm today and dappled shade from the plane trees fell across her. But the whispering leaves sounded like warnings. And the shouts of children playing hide and seek among the trees made her jumpy.

It was an anxious wait until Piotr got there too. 'Andrew can't come,' he said. 'His mum has a doctor's appointment this afternoon and he has to wait with her.' He sat on the wooden slats that formed the back of the bench.

Opposite, the lights were on and the faded sign read 'OPEN'. They could make out movement inside, but they were too far away to see what Omar was up to. The minutes crept past as they waited for Flora. They couldn't do anything without her. They barely spoke. Minnie lolled back against the warm wood. She pulled out her phone. Checked her messages – nothing. Checked the time. Flora had been ages.

'Do you think Sylvie has stopped her coming?' Minnie asked, 'because I didn't apologise well enough?'

'Don't worry. She'll be here.'

But it was another hour of anxiously watching the shop before Minnie heard a rustling, panting sound. She twisted to see Flora racing towards them across the theatre square. She held a huge, pink, frothy dress wrapped in cellophane.

'Am I too late? Did anything happen?' Flora asked. 'I'm sorry, Mum didn't want me to come. She said I had to do my French conversation class. I said "*Maman*, this is *plus important* than learning to *parlez Français*" and she said I was a Philistine. Negotiation took a while. I've had to promise to do extra tuition later, which is a shame because I wanted to finish my book about beetles. Did you know you can tell how long a body has been buried by the types of beetle there are in the remains?' Flora dropped onto the bench with an exhausted sigh.

'What are you reading?' Minnie asked in horror.

'*Forensic Archaeology: An Introduction*, by Professor John Hunter.'

'Well, stop it, it's weird,' Minnie said firmly.

Flora laughed. 'Sorry.'

'What's with the dress?' Piotr asked, looking at the exploded meringue of fabric in disgust.

'Me and Sylvie were bridesmaids for my mum's cousin,' Flora said. 'People ask you to do that sort of thing a lot when you're a twin. I didn't keep my dress, it was too ugly. But Sylvie still pretends to be a princess in hers. I've borrowed it. This is my plan for getting inside the dry cleaner's. I'll need a distraction from you two though once I'm in. You need to get Omar away from the counter somehow.'

It was all very well to say that, Minnie thought, but how were they actually going to do it? Especially if they didn't want Omar to see them?

'Leave it to us,' Piotr said firmly.

Had he a plan? Or was he just trying to sound tough?

Flora carried her dress draped over her forearms like a priest's surplice. She looked left, then right, then left again as she crossed the road.

Then she disappeared into the dry cleaner's.

'So,' Minnie asked Piotr. 'What's your plan?'

Chapter Twenty-Six

Piotr grinned at Minnie. 'You don't believe I have one, do you?'

Minnie sincerely hoped he had, otherwise they had just sent Flora into the lion's den with the lion very much at home.

'Omar's van is back.' Piotr pointed to a white van parked on the street in front of them. 'And there's a red flashing light on the dashboard, see?'

Minnie could just see a little LED beside the steering wheel.

'Well,' Piotr continued, 'that is a car alarm. What would you do if your van alarm suddenly went off in the middle of the day for no reason?'

Minnie grinned. 'I'd come running out of my shop to see whether my van was being stolen or not!'

'Exactly.'

'How do we make it go off?' Minnie asked. She didn't want to smash a window, or do anything that might bring the SOCO team.

'A good shove will usually do it,' Piotr said. 'I've kicked enough footballs at cars by mistake to know that. You ready?'

Minnie nodded.

Piotr launched himself off the bench and ran towards the van. He ducked down behind it. Minnie was right beside him in moments. They crouched low, keeping the broad side of the van between them and the shop front. The traffic trundled past alongside them, sending fumes and dust in their general direction. Minnie covered her nose.

'Put your back into it, on three,' Piotr whispered.

Minnie spun around so that her back was resting against the van's side panel. She laid both palms on its grimy surface. She could feel the grit under the pads of her fingertips.

'One, two, three, *shove*!'

Minnie landed her weight on the van at the exact same moment as Piotr. The van shook violently. Immediately, a high-pitched wail went up.

Waah! Waah! Waah!

'Move!' Piotr grabbed Minnie's hand and dashed across the road between a narrow gap in the traffic. The van was still blaring out angrily.

'This way!' Piotr leaped behind a tree, making the small child who was standing there, counting, jump.

'Are you "it"?' Piotr asked.

The child nodded.

'Well, time's up. Go look for the others.'

The child nodded obediently, then yelled, 'Coming, ready or not!' at the top of her lungs and scampered away.

Minnie and Piotr pressed themselves close to the bark, then peered around at the van.

It was still shrieking. A few pedestrians looked at it, mildly curious, but there was no movement from the dry cleaner's.

'Come on,' Piotr whispered, 'come out.'

Minnie gripped the tree trunk. She willed Omar to leave the shop, to just move, get out!

Just as she could stand it no more, a figure appeared in the doorway. Omar. His white coat whipped around him as he trotted over to his van. They heard a keypad chirrup and the alarm went silent. Omar stalked around the vehicle, checking the bodywork for dents or scratches. He rested his hand on the bonnet and gave it a little pat, as though it were an obedient dog.

Then a second figure appeared at the door. Smaller, redder. Flora.

She had something stuffed up her top.

Had Omar seen?

His hand was still on the bonnet, but one step back towards the pavement and he'd see Flora and her bulge.

'We need to do something!' Minnie said desperately.

Piotr picked up a loose stone, waited until a bus had passed, then hurled it as hard as he could towards the van. It pinged loudly off the broad side.

'Oi!' Omar rushed round to have a look. He ran his hand along the paintwork then glared at the passing bus.

It was just enough time.

While he looked right, Flora darted left. She raced along the road, past the gallery and the grill house in a matter of seconds, her thin legs as speedy as a gazelle's.

'She can run!' Minnie said in admiration.

'So can we. Let's see what she's stuffed up her jumper!'

They weaved between the plane trees, putting more distance between them and Omar. Soon they were by the market. Flora was forced to stop running. She dropped against a wall. Her face was flushed bright pink, with strands of copper hair plastered to her forehead.

'You OK?' Minnie asked.

Flora nodded. She was too out of breath to speak. Instead, she reached under her top and pulled out a bundle of green fabric.

'The T-shirt!' Minnie said.

Flora grinned. 'Stitch,' she said between gasps. She held it up by the shoulders. It was smaller than Minnie remembered. Up close it smelled, ever so slightly, of spices and grime. It had the streets of Lagos in its weave.

'I was too far away to read the label,' Flora said. 'And when Omar ran out of the shop, I didn't know how much time I'd have. So I just grabbed it right off the rack. I stole it!'

'You did the right thing,' Piotr said.

'Let's see the label,' Minnie said.

Flora flipped the neck of the T-shirt. A white receipt with the ace of spades logo was pinned to the seam.

'Someone paid for it to be cleaned. Someone took it from the boy,' Minnie said. 'Does it say who?'

Flora read the label quickly. Then she nodded. 'Yes,' she said. 'It does.'

Chapter Twenty-Seven

'Who?' Piotr asked, desperate to know what the label said.

'Indoors,' Minnie warned. 'We need to get out of sight.'

Minnie led Flora and Piotr into the salon. Two customers were sitting in front of the mirrors. Mum and Bernice worked on their hair, plaiting and smoothing and oiling and fixing. All four women were talking too much to do any more than give a friendly 'Hello!' to the children, before returning to their gossip.

Minnie sat in the window seat, with Flora beside her. Piotr pulled up a stool from the nail bar.

'So?' Minnie asked. 'What does it say?'

Flora laid the T-shirt across her lap and smoothed out its edges gently. Then she lifted the label. ' "Charge to account – Swift Limited," ' she read.

'Is that it?' Minnie asked.

'That's it,' Flora said. 'It tells us who's paying for the cleaning. And whoever is paying for the T-shirt to be cleaned is behind the whole operation – you can always follow the money, that's what it says in books, anyway.'

'Swift Limited? Is that a company?' Piotr asked, surprised. 'I was sure it would be Marcus.'

'Perhaps Marcus *is* Swift Limited,' Flora suggested.

Minnie looked at the flat piece of clothing on Flora's lap. If Flora was right, then they would find the peanut boy and the head of the king in the same place. They could rescue him and stop the head being sold off like some knick-knack at the same time.

Flora took her phone from her backpack and tapped the screen. 'There is a listing for Swift Limited, but not a proper website. It's just a business address. It doesn't say anything about them.'

'Except where they are! We can go there. We can find him!' Minnie said in excitement.

'Yes. It's on the industrial estate, just beyond the railway station,' Flora said.

'Well, that's where we need to go,' Minnie said.

'We can't go without Andrew. Can you imagine what he'd say if we did?'

'Massive wobbly alert,' Minnie agreed. 'Fine. We'll wait a few hours, he'll be done then.'

'What about Sylvie?' Piotr asked.

Minnie pressed her lips together. She still had a funny feeling that her call to Sylvie hadn't gone as well as it should.

'She might join us after her acting class,' Flora said softly. 'It will be getting dark if we wait.'

'Even better,' Minnie replied.

Chapter Twenty-Eight

In the north of the town, a phone rang.

'Badger One, this is Ace One.'

'I told you not to call.'

'I know, boss, but the thing is, the T-shirt's gone. Nicked. Some kid's been poking around.'

'Who?'

'Red-headed girl. She left a bridesmaid's dress behind.'

'You idiot!'

'Yeah, but the thing is, her name is sewn on a tag inside the dress.'

Chapter Twenty-Nine

Piotr and Flora left the salon, Piotr to talk to Andrew, Flora to try and catch Sylvie between classes. A tiny, teeny part of Minnie felt a bit sorry for Sylvie – it wasn't right to have to go to lessons in the holidays. Not that she would ever say that to Sylvie.

The afternoon dragged. She tried to read. But images of the peanut boy swam in front of her eyes – the boy alone on the plane, lost at the airport, frightened when he realised he had the wrong bag. Had the gang hurt him? She put her book down. She clambered on to Gran's bed and looked out of the window. The road was emptier now. The market had packed up and the shopfronts were shuttered like prison cells. A street sweeper drove his whirring machine at walking pace along the gutter. A few people carried shopping bags with last-minute groceries inside. Everyone was headed home.

The flat was strangely quiet. But then, nothing there felt normal at the moment. Mum and Dad had been snapping at each other like Hungry Hippos. Gran wandered around, seeming much smaller than her size, as though she were fading away. Minnie had the feeling that no one wanted to be in the flat at all really. Which was just horrible.

She drew the curtains sharply. Then went to see who was home. Maybe they could keep her mind off the boy until it was time to meet the others. Dad and Gran were in the living room. The telly was on too quietly. It was hard to hear the news. It was as though even the screen were tiptoeing around, worried about intruding. A woman was whispering about a train derailment, an MP taking money they shouldn't have, a hospital in trouble.

The news was depressing. Minnie didn't know why anyone would ever watch it. But Dad and Gran sat staring at it as though it was the most interesting thing ever.

'Tea-time soon,' Dad said without looking away from the screen. 'Go wash your hands.'

Minnie did as she was told. The pipes in the bathroom clanged. Mum must be using the kitchen taps – the boiler couldn't cope with two taps running at once. Which made washing hair in the salon squeally sometimes.

When Minnie went back to the living room, Mum was there too. She stood blocking the doorway, so Minnie waited in the hall behind her.

'I've had a long day,' Mum said. 'Takeout all right for tea?'

Dad grunted.

'I can cook,' Gran said. She pushed herself up heavily.

'No,' Mum said, 'you're our guest. Sit.'

Gran frowned.

'She's not a guest,' Minnie said from the hallway, 'she's family. She lives here now.'

Mum glanced at Dad, who was still watching the news. 'Of course she's family. But she's a guest too. Joseph!'

Dad snapped his eyes away from the screen.

'Tell your mother.'

'What?'

'That she's not to cook.'

Dad looked confused. 'I thought we were having a takeaway?'

Mum threw up her hands and tutted. 'Are you listening? I'll cook. It's fine. I'm sure we've got something in I can use.' She swept past Minnie, who had to duck out of the way, and stormed into the kitchen. They could all hear the clatter of pans being dropped heavily on to the stove.

Dad got up slowly from the sofa and barely glanced at Minnie as he passed her in the hall.

'Taiwo,' he said at the kitchen door, 'leave that. We'll get a takeout.'

'No!' Mum snapped. 'I just wish you'd pay attention to what is happening around you. This is hard, you know, Joseph.'

Minnie sidled closer. She didn't want to hear the row, but she couldn't stop herself listening. It was like picking at a scab and making it bleed again.

Dad reached to take a pan from Mum's hand. She snatched it away. 'Leave it.'

Dad stood rigid, without speaking.

Minnie turned away. She rested her palms on the cool paintwork. Mum and Dad hadn't bickered before. But now that everyone was crammed in and trying to be on their best behaviour in front of Gran, they were arguing more and more.

She went into the living room and sat down beside Gran. She leaned her head against the solid bulk of Gran's shoulder. They could both hear the sniping coming from the kitchen, although Mum and Dad were trying to whisper.

'A third adult in the house is a mistake,' Gran said.

'What? No!' Minnie hadn't liked the idea of sharing a

room with Gran, but now that she was it was cool. Gran was interesting! She didn't want her to go.

Gran wrapped an arm around Minnie and held her tight. 'You're a good girl. And my son is a good son. And my daughter-in-law is a good girl too. But there is no home for me here. The tea knew.' Gran gave a sad little chuckle. 'I should have listened to the tea.'

She kissed Minnie softly, then rose, pressing her hand into the armrest to help herself up.

'Where are you going?'

'I don't know,' Gran said.

Minnie was left alone in the living room. She picked at the fuzzy strip that edged the armrest. Bits of green fluff came away under her nails. She'd thought that all she had to do tonight was slip out and rescue peanut boy and stop an art smuggling gang. But home needed help too. Gran needed to feel safe, to feel wanted. Mum and Dad needed to stop sniping at each other and have some fun.

Minnie smiled.

Babysitting.

She rushed into the kitchen with a huge grin spread across her face.

Mum and Dad were still hovering around the stove. The pans were still empty. Nothing had been resolved.

'You should go out tonight!' Minnie said. 'You need it. You haven't been out together for ages and ages! I think that you should see Gran living here as an opportunity, not a problem. She's not a guest, she's not a visitor to be tiptoed around. She's my gran. And she can look after me so that you can go out and dance. You should be making the most of it, not moping around getting angry at each other.'

They both looked wary, but interested.

'Dad, Mum, please. She just wants to feel wanted.'

'Dancing?' Mum repeated the word as though it were in a foreign language.

'Yes! Dancing!'

Dad looked at Mum. 'What do you think, Taiwo? A bit of time off, eh?'

'And what about food? Tea for everyone?'

'You can eat out,' Minnie said. 'I'll make sandwiches for me and Gran.'

'Sandwiches?' Mum said.

'It will be fine,' Minnie insisted. 'You should have some fun for a change.'

'The girl has a point,' Dad said. 'Maybe we do need to let our hair down.'

'What, now?' Mum looked as bemused as if a penguin had waddled in and put the kettle on.

'Why not? We used to be impulsive. Do you remember?' Dad wrapped his arm around Mum's waist and pulled her into a spin. 'We used to take off at a moment's notice and stay up to watch the sunrise.'

'We did, didn't we?'

'Go on,' Minnie said, waving at Mum. 'Go and put a dress on. And some lipstick.'

Mum smiled. 'Give me two minutes.'

It did only take two minutes. Mum pulled on her favourite dancing dress, with a red skirt that flared when she twirled. She ran lipstick around her mouth and pressed her lips closed over a tissue. Done.

Dad was right behind her. He tugged on a clean shirt and his polished black shoes. There was an air of excitement in the flat now, like Christmas Eve.

Gran opened her bedroom door to see what all the noise was about and smiled. 'You two are so handsome!' she said.

'You don't mind us going out?' Mum asked.

'Go!' Gran said. 'While I'm still here to help.'

Mum dropped a quick kiss on Minnie's head. 'You're a good girl. Thank you.' Then they were gone. Minnie smiled, but Gran's words to Mum made her feel prickly and weird. One evening of having a job to do wasn't enough to make Gran feel she had a role here. But Minnie wanted her to stay. She wanted Gran to feel safe and comfortable and at home.

And it was Swift Limited's fault that she didn't.

Minnie made two sandwiches in the kitchen and carried a plate through to Gran.

It was down to her to stop Gran from leaving, to save peanut boy, to save the king of Ife. But first she needed to get permission to go out.

'I thought I might go out to see Sylvie,' Minnie said. 'I won't be out late. Mum lets me sometimes, as long as I don't have homework.'

'Does she?' Gran asked. 'Well, Sylvie is such a very nice girl.'

Yuck. Gran was right about lots of things, but not about that.

'What time will you be home?'

'I'll just be gone an hour,' Minnie said, hoping that would be enough time.

Gran raised her head and looked out of the window. Warm evening sunshine was thrown across the street outside like a gold sari. 'Be back before dark.'

Minnie grinned.

It was the perfect evening to rescue a missing boy.

Chapter Thirty

The main railway line ran across town, tucked behind terraced gardens and potting sheds. Its embankments rose like ancient fortifications. The line itself snaked over archways into the station, where it branched into platforms: long concrete streaks where people stood sipping coffee.

Beyond the station, most of the lines came together again and shot off towards the next town. They ran parallel with metal boxy buildings, tangles of brambles and buddleia and barbed wire fences – the industrial estate.

Minnie rushed towards the station and waited impatiently for Andrew and Piotr – she had called them before leaving the flat. Flora had texted to say she was on her way.

There were a few late stragglers on their way home from work, but rush hour was well and truly over. The air was heavy and warm, the slow pace of evening taking over.

'Hey!' Andrew bounced into view, followed by Piotr.

'How's your mum?' Minnie asked.

Andrew gave an orange segment smile. 'Good. The doctor's happy. She's at home tucked up in front of re-runs of *Casualty*.'

'She doesn't mind you being out?'

'We're both allowed as long as we stay together,' Piotr said. 'And get home before dark. What about Flora and Sylvie?'

Minnie pointed back down the hill – Flora was skipping to meet them, her backpack bouncing and jangling. No Sylvie. Oh.

'My dad has his office on the industrial estate,' Flora said as she rushed up to greet them. 'I've been there before. There's a map of the whole thing on the way in.'

They made their way towards the estate together, stopping by a neatly trimmed patch of lawn like a miniature golf course. A board, maybe three metres high, was set up beyond the mini lawn. It was a map and a list of all the companies on the estate. There were tech agencies, paper products, office temps, PC repairs, and – there – Swift Limited. It had the smallest sign, right at the bottom of the board. The outline of a bird flew above the company name.

176

'Two of us should go and look while two of us stand guard,' Piotr said.

'I'm going to look,' Minnie said in a voice that meant arguing was pointless.

'Sure,' Piotr said. 'I'll come with you. Flora and Andrew, you can keep watch. Flora, you have your phone?'

Flora nodded.

'Call us if you see anything. Call Jimmy if we don't reply.'

Piotr and Minnie left them by the huge board.

The estate seemed deserted, the offices closed, lights switched off, car parks empty. Minnie felt as though she were in a ghost town. The black windows were like empty eye sockets, watching blindly.

She took a deep breath.

There was no black magic at work. The postcard was a cipher, that was all. And the boy hadn't been taken by witches; he was a little boy who needed their help.

She had to be brave.

It was good that Piotr was walking beside her.

'You OK?' he asked.

She nodded. 'You?'

'Bit scared,' he admitted.

She felt a little better. 'It's going to be all right,' she said hopefully.

Swift Limited was at the end of a drive, fenced off from the other office units with a gate across the access road. The gate was closed. It squealed in protest as they drew back the bolt.

They were inside.

It was a low single-storey building, red brick, metal covers over the windows. The door facing them had a small plaque showing the same bird logo as the board.

'This is it.' Minnie walked up to the door and tried the handle. She hadn't expected the door to open, and it didn't.

She crept to the side of the building – no doors, no windows. Finally, she walked around the back. She could see an emergency exit set in the wall and three tiny windows, all but one completely covered by metal sheets. The building backed on to a high fence. The narrow patch between the wall and the fence was overgrown with nettles and dotted with wind-blown rubbish. It smelled of damp earth and leaves.

'I'm not going down there,' Piotr said. 'Our legs will get stung to death.'

'You've got jeans on, and it's nothing a dock leaf won't fix.'

'OK, just don't spit on the dock leaf first. That's gross.'

They walked carefully, nudging the nettles aside with their feet before treading gently.

'Ow,' Piotr said, as a nettle sprang back up and swiped his hand.

'Shh,' Minnie said.

Just then, one of the small windows opened a fraction. Just a centimetre or two.

Minnie froze. Piotr, sucking at his stung wrist, stopped too.

The window opened wider. A head leaned out.

The head belonged to a young boy with close-cut black hair and skin the warm brown of oak.

'Hello,' the boy said. He had an accent that Minnie recognised instantly. Lagos.

'Hello,' she said.

'What do you want?' the boy asked, his voice nervous.

'My gran saw you on the plane,' Minnie said. 'We know there's a gang who make you deliver messages. Are you all right? Are the gang here now?'

The boy glanced warily over his shoulder. 'I'm on my own, except for the demons.'

'Right,' Minnie said. 'Get back from the window. We're coming in.'

Chapter Thirty-One

Sylvie's acting class was over.

She packed up her plimsolls in a vanity case and washed her face in the bathroom before heading out.

There was warm evening sunshine outside, so instead of calling Mum to ask for a lift, she decided to walk. Her calves ached from dance earlier. She walked on tiptoes to stretch them out. Maybe it was worth calling Mum after all?

She unclipped the clasps on her case and looked for her phone. It wasn't there. Rats. Mum hadn't packed it. Still. It was a nice evening. The walk wasn't far. She'd be home in ten minutes.

She didn't move.

The others were out investigating.

Flora had told her about it earlier, but she hadn't wanted to listen. Minnie's so-called apology still smarted.

The way Minnie had fobbed her off when she'd asked about their plans, it was obvious that Minnie hadn't wanted her. And then Flora had added insult to injury by admitting she'd taken Sylvie's bridesmaid dress without even asking! So Sylvie had been too cross to listen properly. But now ... with the balmy sunshine on her face and her muscles aching pleasantly, Sylvie wondered what the others were doing.

She could almost remember the name of the place Flora had mentioned – Speedy? Quickly? Something like that. She stood on the pavement and looked left and right. The peach sky made the street look golden. It was nice out, but she had no idea where to go.

Great.

Sylvie found half a Mars bar that she'd forgotten about at the bottom of her vanity case. The best thing to do would be to go to the salon or the cafe and see if the others were there. She chewed happily as she made her way to Marsh Road.

She didn't notice a silver car parked on double yellow lines outside the stage school.

Chapter Thirty-Two

Minnie couldn't believe it. She was scrambling up through the window and trying not to land on peanut boy. They'd found him! They'd really found him! She grabbed hold of the flaking window sill and pulled her long legs through. She dropped down on to a chair, then to the floor, with Piotr right behind her.

She looked around.

There was no light on, so the little room she found herself in was gloomy. If she stretched her arms out beside her, she'd be able to touch both walls. The door was opposite the window. There wasn't much furniture – a roll-mat bed, with a wrinkled sleeping bag tossed on to it; the battered teddy bear from the case; a chair with a small pile of comics on the seat; and the suitcase itself, black, scuffed and grained with harmattan dust.

They were in the right place.

'Are you OK?' Piotr asked the boy. 'Are you hurt?'

Minnie looked at him properly.

He was much smaller than Minnie and Piotr – he could only be six or seven years old. His eyes looked huge: black pupils gleaming in the dim light. His face was all eyes. His hair was buzz-cut short, a sprinkling of black on his scalp.

He wore a bright orange T-shirt with a crocodile logo.

He smiled. 'I am not hurt.'

Then Minnie noticed a scab on his lip, crusted and old, but still sore-looking. She pointed at it. 'But you were hurt.'

The boy's fingers rested gently on the scab. 'I got it wrong,' he whispered. 'I took the wrong case.'

Minnie felt a flash of fury. Who would hit a small boy for making a mistake?

She crouched down so that her eyes were level with the boy's. 'I'm Minnie,' she said, 'that's Piotr and we're here to help you. OK? What's your name?'

'Femi,' the boy said. He held out his small hand. Minnie took it and held it. His fingers felt cold.

'Hello, Minnie. Hello, Piotr.' Femi struggled to pronounce Piotr's name. He twisted his tongue around it a few times, then grinned. 'It's a difficult name,' he said.

'Where are your family?' Minnie asked.

Femi shrugged. 'I don't know. I haven't seen them since I was little.'

'How long have you been working for the smugglers?'

'Since I left my home. I stay here sometimes.' He waved at the little room. 'I stay in Lagos sometimes. I like it in Lagos more. I stay with a lot of people. They talk to me. I don't like it here. It's too cold. And there are demons.'

Minnie frowned. He'd said that before. 'Femi, what do you mean, "demons"?'

Chapter Thirty-Three

Sylvie was annoyed to find that the salon was locked and in darkness. There was no sign at all of Flora or Minnie or anyone.

She pressed the buzzer for the flat above the shop.

It sounded for a while. She waited. There was no answer. So she pressed it again.

'Yes? Hello? What?' a confused-sounding voice said. Sylvie recognised it as Minnie's gran.

'Oh, hello, Auntie. This is Sylvie. Is Minnie there?'

Minnie's gran made a little shocked noise, like a squirrel finding his nut store empty. 'She's not with you?'

'No,' Sylvie replied.

'She said she was going to see you.'

'Oh.'

'You're sure she isn't with you?' There was a definite edge of panic in Auntie's voice.

'Sorry, no.'

'Wait there!'

After a few minutes, the light flicked on in the salon. Sylvie saw Auntie rushing across the room, trying to pull on her coat with one arm and get her boot on with the other. She held her handbag with her teeth.

Auntie pulled open the front door and locked it behind her. She dropped her handbag on the floor. 'Little Minnie is missing,' Auntie said. 'And she isn't answering her phone.'

Little Minnie? Sylvie was about to object, then she realised just how frightened Auntie was; the whites of her eyes were like the shores around dark islands.

'It's OK,' Sylvie said. 'I'm sure she's fine. She's probably with my sister.'

Auntie shook her head. 'She didn't say anything about a sister. She said she was going to visit you. Back before dusk. I fell asleep. I should have been watching her. Now something has happened to my little granddaughter.'

All the time, Auntie had been pulling on her coat and doing up the buttons. She hoisted her bag on to her shoulder like a knight pulling on a shield. 'We're going to look for her,' Auntie said firmly.

'Look for her?' Sylvie wondered whether it was too

late to say that she had homework or a dentist appointment, or that Mum really needed her to sort through her sock drawer and put all the pairs in order. *Anything*. But Auntie was staring at her with those lost eyes.

She sighed. She had to help, even though the chances of Minnie actually being in any trouble were somewhere between nothing and zero.

'Well,' Sylvie said. 'If she was going to my house, how about we walk that way and keep an eye out for her? Maybe she's just dawdling and lost track of time.'

Auntie took her arm. 'You're a very good girl, Sylvie.'

Right at that moment, Sylvie had to agree.

At the end of the road, where the pedestrian zone stopped and the traffic began, a silver car started its engine with an expensive roar.

As they walked past, the window on the driver's side whirred down. 'Mrs Adesina!' a voice called. 'I'm so pleased to run into you.'

'Police commissioner?' Mrs Adesina said.

'Hop in. I'll give you a lift.'

Sylvie had never seen the police commissioner before, hadn't even known there was one if she was honest. But the car was very fancy, tinted windows, air conditioning, leather seats. 'We can look out for Minnie just as well from the car as from the pavement,' she said to Auntie, and popped open the back door.

They got into the car.

Chapter Thirty-four

Inside the shed, Femi looked frightened, his skinny arms wrapped around his body. 'I don't like them.'

'Who?' Minnie asked gently.

'The demons,' Femi replied.

'Is it Omar? Marcus?' Minnie asked.

Femi bit his lip, but didn't answer.

From her pocket, Minnie felt the vibration of her phone ringing, then the melody of a call coming in. She pulled her phone out and jammed the mute button. Gran. Probably wondering when she was going to get home. No time for that now. Minnie switched her phone to silent.

'Are they in this building?' Piotr moved to the doorway and listened.

'Can you show us?' Minnie asked, putting her phone away. 'We'll keep you safe, I promise.'

'You'll stay close?' Femi asked.

'Like fleas on a dog.'

Femi nodded reluctantly. 'This way,' he said.

He opened the door. Straight away, Minnie and Piotr noticed the temperature change. The air outside was much colder. Minnie hadn't noticed a heater in Femi's room, so why was it so much colder out here? She could feel goosebumps on her arms. Femi's hand reached for hers.

They were in a short corridor. Opposite was the main door, with a hefty looking square lock. There were two other doors. One was ajar and she could see a small bathroom. The other, at the end of the corridor, was closed.

It was this door that Femi led them towards. He paused in front of it.

Minnie gave his hand a short squeeze. 'It's all right,' she said. She hoped she was telling the truth.

Femi turned the handle and pushed open the door. Minnie and Piotr followed him inside.

The room was dark, entirely dark, and cold: it was like walking into a cave. It smelled like one too, musty and old. She remembered the covered windows she'd seen around the back of the building. They must be inside that space. She could tell from the echoes of their footsteps that the room was large.

Minnie's eyes strained to see in the dark. Eventually she could make out lumps in a different shade of black. A tiny amount of light must have been squeezing in at the windows' edges.

Femi dropped her hand and walked away. 'Where are you going?' she whispered.

'Wait!' his urgent voice replied.

She could hear him patting the walls, scrabbling for something.

Then the room blazed with light. Femi had found the light switch.

Minnie wished he hadn't. Now she knew exactly what he meant by demons.

Heads. Dozens of heads.

They were arranged on rickety shelves. Carved from wood, each one was scarred and maimed: hundreds of nails had been hammered into eye sockets and mouths; rusty screws, barbed wire and tiny saw blades ripped into the wooden flesh; flattened noses had been cut again and again with terrible piercings. Beside them lay metal swords, wooden clubs and shields made from animal skins. A small museum of smuggled objects.

'Demons,' Femi whispered. 'They were just spirits once, but the men say they have become demons. I must behave or they will get me.'

Minnie walked further into the space on tiptoe, almost holding her breath.

There was a man – no, a costume of straw and rope. It stood six foot high, with a long crocodile's snout and sharp slices of metal laid one over another to make jaws stuffed with teeth. Its painted eyes had all the patient menace of an ambush hunter. Tin-can monkeys hung from its limbs.

She had heard of masquerades, but had never seen them. But her cousins had told her about the men who'd take on the form of spirits and chant and dance into the night.

She glanced back at the door. Piotr was inside the room, staring in astonishment, but Femi had retreated to the doorway, his arms folded again.

On the right there was a huge figure covered in coloured grass – pink, blue, orange, green, a rainbow of reeds. But its face wasn't peaceful. Blood red lips glowed in a coal black face, horns rose from its forehead.

'Femi,' Minnie said, 'what is all this?'

'Demons,' he whispered. 'Demons for sale.'

Then Minnie noticed something else tucked into a corner, forgotten. A black suitcase, identical to the one in Femi's room. She moved closer and checked the luggage label. *Mrs Adesina, c/o Beauty Cuts, Marsh Road.*

Gran's case. With her tea inside. And her address attached. The case that had started all this.

Well, now Minnie was going to finish it. 'We're getting out of here,' she said. 'You too, Femi. We're going to end this and the police are going to listen.'

Chapter Thirty-Five

Sylvie slipped into the back seat beside Auntie and closed the car door.

The sounds of the street were immediately gone. The inside of the car was a soundproof, luxurious bubble. It was almost like being in a submarine, cut off from the world outside. Even the tint to the windows made the few people in the street seem odd, like cut-outs from magazines pasted on to the glass, weirdly flat and colourless. Sylvie wondered why a police commissioner wanted to feel so isolated?

'So, Anthea, have you found my suitcase, eh?' Auntie asked.

'Please put your seat belts on,' Anthea said smoothly.

'Or have you found out who broke into our flat?'

Anthea didn't reply. She turned the radio on. Classical music flooded the car from speakers hidden discreetly in the upholstery.

'Ah, Brahms,' the commissioner said.

'What about my case?'

'Why don't you just enjoy the music while I drive?'

'Where are we going?' Sylvie asked. 'We're looking for my friend Minnie. She might be walking to my house. It's the next left.'

Anthea took the next right.

They were headed away from town.

Sylvie looked at Auntie in alarm. Her skin began to prickle. What on earth was going on?

Chapter Thirty-Six

Andrew and Flora sat on the curb underneath the board displaying company names. The sky above them had turned to a violet twilight. Flora tucked her arms under her knees to keep them warm.

'They've been gone for ages,' Andrew said.

'I know.'

'Do you think they're all right? Do you think they found the boy?'

'I don't know.'

'Tell me something interesting to keep me distracted,' Andrew said.

Flora thought for a moment. 'Did you know the Chinese were the first civilisation to use fingerprint analysis? They used to sign contracts with an inky thumb because everyone's thumb print is different. That way you couldn't say you hadn't agreed to something if you changed your mind later.'

Andrew pressed his thumb into the dirt at the edge of the road and then stamped Flora's arm with it.

'Hey!' she said.

Andrew laughed. 'Sorry, I just couldn't –' Suddenly silent, his head shot up.

'What?' Flora asked.

'Listen,' he whispered.

Flora listened.

Whistling.

They both scrabbled to their feet and ducked behind the board, where there were wooden struts running horizontally. They lifted themselves on to these, so that their feet wouldn't show below.

The whistling was closer. Someone was very pleased with life.

Flora noticed a small hole where a screw had fallen out. She peeped through.

A tall someone in a white suit was strolling down the drive. Marcus.

'We have to warn Minnie and Piotr,' she whispered. 'Marcus is headed towards them.'

'Marcus?' Andrew glowered at the back of the wooden board. 'I never liked him, not from the moment I laid eyes on him.'

'Shh.'

He was parallel with them now. If he glanced in their direction, he would see them clinging to the back of the sign.

Flora willed him to carry on walking, not to look. She clung tighter to the splintery wood of the struts, desperate not to make the slightest sound.

Marcus walked right past.

As soon as he was twenty metres away, they dropped down on to the grass without a sound and tiptoed to the far side of the board, out of sight.

Flora scrabbled in her bag. Book, keys, purse – she was feeling all the wrong shapes. Then her fingers felt something smooth and hard – phone! She pulled it out and texted rapidly. Send!

She just hoped Minnie got the message in time to get out of there.

Chapter Thirty-Seven

Inside the warehouse, Minnie and Piotr stood in the middle of the room of demons. All around, from the shelves, blank eyes stared back, knotted hair rose in stiff spikes, faces slashed with gouged marks or pierced with iron and bronze watched them.

'How long has this been going on? Femi, how many times have you carried messages?'

She looked at the small boy. He looked down at the ground. He bit his knuckle. 'Lots. I don't know how many,' he whispered.

So, it wasn't just the head of the king that had been smuggled into the country. There were artefacts and objects all around them that didn't belong in a dark, dingy warehouse. It wasn't right. 'Where do they all come from?' she asked.

Femi looked down at the ground. 'Bad men,' he whispered.

'It's a network,' Piotr said. 'It must be to have moved so many objects. Men in Lagos steal the art and send it here. Then Femi carries a message to tell Marcus where and when to collect it. Marcus makes money when he sells it on.'

Femi nodded. 'The men are very happy when I take back my case.'

'Because it's got money in it?'

Minnie didn't wait for a reply. She had noticed something at the end of a shelf. An object wrapped in cloth. Cloth she had seen before, at the railway station.

She walked towards it, her hands held out. She grasped it. It was surprisingly heavy for something so small, like carrying a jug full of water. She lifted it over to an empty steel table. 'We need the evidence for Jimmy,' she said. 'I'm going to photograph everything, then he'll have to listen to us.' She pulled out her phone and glanced at the screen. The missed call from Gran was still there. And a text. From Flora. She gasped.

'What is it?' Piotr asked.

'Marcus is on his way!'

'We have to get out of here!' Piotr turned back the way they'd come.

'Wait!' Minnie said. 'I need to photograph this.'

'There's no time!'

'Wait!' she said again. She moved aside the waxed cloth, like unwrapping a yearned for present, careful not to bump or jolt the thing underneath.

Piotr was at her side. 'Minnie, we have to get out of here.'

Femi watched the doorway anxiously.

'I'll be one second,' Minnie said. She knew Piotr was right. There was no time. But she couldn't just walk out of here without any evidence. This had to end now.

The cloth fell back and revealed the head beneath. The metal was flaked with shades of brown, amber, copper, black, like skin reflecting sunlight. The cheeks were marked, corduroy ridges running straight down: the scars of old cuts that decorated the king. She could imagine blood running down the king's face, him biting his lips together to stop from crying out as the marks were made. She held his cheeks in the palms of her hands, her thumbs resting either side of his beetle-wing nostrils. The beaded crown rose high above his forehead.

'What are you doing?' Piotr said. 'Leave it. We have to go.'

But they were too late. They all heard the sound of a key sliding into the front door.

Piotr and Minnie looked at each other in horror. Femi ran from the room, back into his little bedroom and closed the door.

They were on their own and about to get caught.

Unless they found a way out.

Minnie scanned the room. There was no other exit. The windows were all covered.

Hiding?

There were no cupboards or beds to hide under – just shelves of weird heads and costumes.

'The masquerades!' she hissed at Piotr. She flung the waxed fabric back over the king's head and raced towards the crocodile costume.

Piotr understood. He headed for the reeded rainbow devil.

The crocodile was enveloped in a long straw skirt that reached down to the ground. Minnie parted the straw, as though pulling aside a curtain, and ducked inside. It was a tight squeeze. She crouched there and let the straw fall back into place.

She heard rustling as Piotr slipped inside the rainbow spirit.

Minnie smelled sweat and warm grass. Her nose tickled. She forced back a sneeze.

'Femi!' an angry voice called from the corridor. 'What have I told you about going into the storage space?'

Then there were footsteps coming closer.

'The light is on. And things have been moved.'

Minnie heard a door open slowly. Then Femi's voice, so soft she could hardly hear. 'I'm sorry.'

'You don't listen, hmm? Is that it? What happens to little boys who don't listen?' the man's voice had a steely edge. Minnie recognised Marcus's voice at once.

'Demons eat him.'

'That's right, the demons will eat him. The masquerades will wake and wonder who it was that roused them from slumber. They hate to be woken. They're crotchety at the very best of times. One of them might just decide that there's nothing more satisfying for breakfast than an irritating small boy. Then, *chomp, chomp, chomp*, no more Femi.'

Minnie peered through the straw. Femi was slumped miserably – his head hung low and his shoulders were clenched right to his ears.

The poor boy. Stuck in here, in the dark, frightened all the time. And all for money, for the profit they could make from selling stolen art. It wasn't right. It was pathetic to frighten a child like that. Pathetic and wrong.

Minnie clenched her fists.

The grass skirt rustled.

Femi gasped.

'What?' Marcus asked.

'The masquerades are waking,' Femi whispered.

'Nonsense,' Marcus said.

Did his voice waver? Minnie was sure she'd heard fear there, just for a second.

She knew he was a man with a love of words. A man given to wild ideas. Was he really only trying to scare Femi? Or was a tiny part of him scared of the masquerades too?

She deliberately rustled the skirt again.

Femi burst into tears. She'd have to apologise to him later.

Marcus grabbed the boy and shoved him towards the crocodile. 'See what it is. It's probably just a mouse. Go, take a look.'

Minnie grabbed the wooden bar that ran up to the crocodile's head and straightened up.

The whole costume rose off the ground. The leering jaws of the crocodile clattered above her head.

Femi screamed and ran towards the door.

Marcus stepped back. 'Who are you? Who's there? I don't believe you're real. I don't.'

Then the rainbow spirit got to his feet. The huge horns on the top of his head scraped against the ceiling tiles.

Marcus screamed. He backed away.

But Femi had slammed the door; Marcus was alone with the demons!

The rainbow spirit took a step forwards. Minnie found a lever that operated the crocodile's mouth. Its jaws rattled like dry bones.

Marcus's face was drained pale. Sweat glistened on his forehead.

Minnie clattered the crocodile's jaw again. She stepped left and right, herding Marcus in a fearful dance. Piotr did the same, both of them closing in, penning him in.

Marcus raced desperately to a window. They were shut tight. He wheeled around, looking for anything to use to protect himself.

He reached wildly for the objects on the nearest shelf: he grabbed and dropped a wooden mask; he grabbed and dropped a metal bowl; he grabbed a steel sword –

And didn't drop it.

He turned to face the two masquerades.

He pointed his sword right at Minnie. 'Don't come any closer,' he said. 'Or, I swear, I'll use this.'

Chapter Thirty-Eight

Sylvie was watching the world race by a little too fast. The police commissioner was listening to the music swelling from the speakers and paid no attention to the passengers in the back seat.

Sylvie did not like this journey one bit. She didn't know where they were going or why.

She looked around for clues. They were heading out of town, in the direction of the hospital. Why would this woman be taking them there?

'How well do you know the police commissioner?' Sylvie hissed to Auntie, who was looking more confused than frightened.

'Oh, me and Anthea Swift had a very long conversation once,' Auntie said.

Something about that sentence caught Sylvie's attention, like a fish catching on a line, pulling it taut.

Swift.

That was the name Flora had mentioned earlier. Not Speedy. Not Quickly. Swift Limited.

The company behind the art smuggling ring.

Suddenly so many things fell into place. The reason why no proper police investigation had taken place. Why Auntie hadn't heard from Jimmy at all. Someone in the police department was making sure it wasn't investigated. And that someone was driving them away in a car.

Sylvie gestured to Auntie, tapping her thumb to her palm, keeping her hand low, out of sight. Would Auntie understand? Would she know what Sylvie was trying to signal?

Auntie seemed to get it. She patted herself down gingerly. Then she reached gently into her handbag which was next to her on the seat. She pulled out a phone and slipped it to Sylvie.

Well done, Auntie!

Sylvie needed to text for help. If she called, Anthea would be on to her in a second.

Could you text 999? Sylvie had no idea.

The best person to text would be Jimmy, but she didn't know his number. She didn't know Flora's either.

She had a horrible realisation that she was going to

have to text someone who was already on Auntie's phone. There weren't going to be many options.

She pressed a button on the keypad.

The phone beeped!

'What was that?' Anthea asked.

Argh! Auntie hadn't switched off her keypad sounds. Who did that? Old people.

'What was that beep?' Anthea demanded again, craning her head, looking at them in the rear-view mirror.

There was no choice. Sylvie was just going to have to type fast and furious and hope she got the message away in time. *Here goes nothing*, she thought.

HELP, she typed – *beep, beep, beep, beep* – 'in pcs car. S.' *Beep, beep, beep, beep* …

'What are you doing?' Anthea yelled.

Sylvie clicked Minnie's number and hit 'Send'.

Anthea pulled hard right into a lay-by. The car stopped. Sylvie yanked the door handle. It wouldn't open! Child locks. She leaned over Auntie and grabbed the handle on her side. Locked too!

Anthea was out of the car. She wrenched open Sylvie's door, reached in, snatched the phone and threw it into the road.

A lorry rolled right over it and crushed it to smithereens.

'My phone!' Auntie yelled.

'That's the least of your worries.' Anthea slammed the door.

Sylvie cradled her wrist. It hurt.

This was scary now.

Anthea got back into the driver's seat and edged the car back into the lane of traffic. She smoothed her hair flat in the rear-view mirror and dabbed at her lipstick with her index finger. She looked cool and poised again.

'Well,' she said, 'that wasn't very clever. Not very clever at all.'

Sylvie pressed herself into the leather seat. She couldn't get far enough away from the woman in the front.

Auntie leaned forward. 'That phone was a gift from my son!'

'All I wanted was a chat,' Anthea said, ignoring Auntie completely, 'and you had to go and pull a stunt like that.'

'A chat about what?' Sylvie said fiercely.

Anthea's red slash lips frowned for a second. 'You know what about. There's no point pretending. You took something. An item of clothing. My fool of an associate left some embarrassing evidence that I would like back.'

Sylvie shook her head. 'I've nothing of yours,' she said.

'It will do you no good. Swift Limited is being cleared as we speak. In an hour there will be nothing there to find. But I would like the T-shirt back, just to be certain. You were in the dry cleaner's. You took it. I want it back.'

The dry cleaner's? Sylvie had never been anywhere near it. She hadn't even seen the T-shirt.

But she knew who had.

Flora.

Anthea thought that she was Flora. Anthea was driving the wrong twin!

Chapter Thirty-Nine

Andrew and Flora watched Marcus go into the warehouse. They waited anxiously for Minnie and Piotr to come sprinting towards them.

But there was nothing.

Then from inside the building came the sound of screams.

'He's hurting them!' Flora shrieked. She bolted to the front door and tugged hard at the handle, but it was locked from the inside.

Andrew was at her side, both of them pulling the door, rattling it in its frame. It didn't budge.

She banged the door with the flats of her palms. 'Let us in! Let us in!'

Andrew pulled her away. 'Flora! Let's try the back.'

Just then the door opened.

They looked up, then down.

A small boy was looking back up at them. They'd found the peanut boy!

'Have you come to stop the demons?' he asked in a small voice.

'Yes,' Andrew said firmly. 'We have.'

'Good, because Uncle Marcus has got a sword. But I don't think swords will work on demons, do you? And she'll be angry if the demons hurt Uncle Marcus.'

Flora and Andrew stepped into the darkness of the warehouse.

Flora didn't know how she was going to stop demons, but this shivering whippet of a boy needed her to try. So she was going to.

The boy pulled her along a narrow corridor, dark on all sides, then into a big room where two terrifying creatures rattled and clacked, and all around were shelves of heads, nailed, hammered, warped – heads looking back at her. Flora gasped. Demons?

Demons fighting Marcus. The two moving creatures were monstrous, huge. Marcus was backed into a corner. He did, indeed, have a sword, which he was pointing at the upright crocodile.

The little boy whimpered miserably.

'You stay back!' Marcus yelled. He swung the sword wildly; the blade flashed under the clinical strip light, like a surgeon's scalpel.

The crocodile jerked away from the slashing metal.

Flora didn't know what to do. Demons? Really? Should she help Marcus? Get the boy out of there?

'Demons?' Andrew said, standing by her side. 'Not in those trainers. Oi! You two. You'll need this.' Andrew grabbed something from a nearby shelf – a wood and leather shield. He threw it across the room to the crocodile.

The crocodile turned at the sound of Andrew's voice. Its arms shot up to catch the shield and Flora caught a flash of brown hand, pink sleeve – Minnie! It was Minnie inside the costume. And Marcus was waving a sword at her!

Minnie spun back to face Marcus, who stood with the sword held high. The metal gleamed. He brought it down hard.

At the same moment Minnie swung her shield like a cricket bat and caught Marcus hard on the jaw. The sword clattered to the floor.

The rainbow creature – who, Flora realised, must be Piotr – jumped on to Marcus's back. The two fell to the ground. Minnie launched herself forward too, shield and all, and landed on the gallery owner with a yell of triumph.

'Andrew!' Flora said. 'Find some rope, or something to tie him up with!'

She and Andrew scoured the shelves. There was nothing. Then Andrew gave a cry and held up some thick brown packing tape.

The wriggling figures were doing an excellent job of holding Marcus down. The weight of the costumes was more than enough to keep him pinned to the floor, let alone the weight of the two people inside them.

Flora kicked the sword away and passed the tape to Minnie. In seconds, Marcus's hands were secured behind his back and his ankles were packing-taped together.

Minnie stood up and pulled the crocodile head off. She was sweaty, but smiling. 'We've done it!' she said. 'We found the boy and we found the stolen art! We did it!'

Marcus rolled on the floor like a human sausage roll. Then he met Flora's gaze and froze. He looked confused, then panicked. 'You shouldn't be here,' he whispered.

Minnie, Piotr and Andrew didn't hear. They were too busy whooping with joy that they had solved the case and saved Femi. Minnie got out of the costume and picked up Femi. She twirled him around like a carousel horse.

But Flora didn't celebrate. She felt a stab of worry. She stood over Marcus, looking down at him. 'What do you mean?' she asked. 'Why shouldn't I be here?'

Marcus shook his head. He clamped his lips tight. He wasn't going to say anything.

There was something else bothering her, too, like the beginning of toothache. Something Femi had said. She turned to him. Minnie had stopped spinning, but was still holding the little boy.

'Femi,' Flora said, 'when we came in you said that *she* would be angry if the demons hurt Marcus. Who is *she*?'

Femi frowned. 'The boss, of course.'

The boss? Marcus wasn't the boss?

The celebrating fizzled out as they all realised what Femi had said.

This wasn't over.

'We should call the police,' Piotr said.

'No!' Femi cried. 'No police! Uncle Marcus says the police are worse than the demons.'

Minnie put Femi down, crouched in front of him and took both his hands in hers. 'You've done nothing wrong,' she said. 'It's Marcus who should be frightened of the police, not you. The police can help you find your family again. Would you like that?'

'My family?' Femi's sliver of a smile was painful to watch. 'I'd like to see my family,' he whispered.

Minnie pulled out her phone. 'I'll call Jimmy,' she said. She looked at the screen and gasped.

Chapter Forty

'This is bad,' Minnie said, looking at her phone. 'Bad, bad, bad.'

'Let me go!' Marcus said, rolling on the concrete floor of the storeroom, collecting dust and smears on his smart suit.

Everyone ignored him.

Flora stepped closer to Minnie and peered at her phone. 'What is it?'

Minnie bit her lip. She looked at Flora, who seemed paler than usual, frightened. She was right to be. 'A text,' Minnie said, 'from Gran's phone. But I don't think Gran sent it.'

'What does it say?' Andrew asked.

'It says: *HELP in pcs car. S.*'

'Who's S?' Andrew asked.

'Sylvie,' Flora whispered.

'Who's pcs?' Andrew asked.

They looked at each other. Sylvie needed them; she was in trouble. But with who?

'Pc might be police constable?' Piotr suggested. 'Maybe she's with Jimmy.'

Flora shook her head. 'Sylvie knows he's a special constable. And why would she be asking for help if she was with Jimmy? I don't like this!' Her voice rose and almost cracked with worry. 'Where's Sylvie? Where's my sister?'

'And my gran,' Minnie said flatly. Sylvie was using Gran's phone. That wasn't good.

'Don't panic,' Piotr said. He was out of the masquerade. 'Flora, do you have your notebook?'

Flora pulled off her backpack and nodded.

'Have we any suspects, anyone who might be pcs? Any initials or places? Or companies? Anything at all?'

Flora unzipped her bag. She pulled out the green T-shirt and laid it on the table, then she took out her notebook and opened it. Minnie saw flashes of their investigation – the postcard, interviews with the window cleaner, the Nigerian letterhead. But no pcs.

Nothing.

'My T-shirt!' Femi said in delight.

Minnie picked it up to give to him. Then she paused. He looked up at her, one hand on the T-shirt she was still holding. 'Femi,' Minnie said. 'What do you know about the boss? Have you ever seen her? Do you know her name? It's important. The lady who noticed you on the plane, who accidentally took your case, she's my gran. My family. And she's in trouble. Anything you can tell us might help us find her. Oh, and Sylvie, Flora's sister.'

Femi frowned deeply, thinking. 'I don't know her name.'

'What does she look like?'

He shrugged again. 'I don't know. She doesn't come here.'

'Please, Femi, anything you can remember might help.'

Andrew coughed. She looked up. He was standing near Marcus. He held the sword that Marcus had been waving around only moments ago. Andrew raised an eyebrow. 'I bet I can get Marcus to tell us.' He lifted the sword.

'Andrew!' Minnie snapped. 'No one gets hurt. Yet. Give Femi a chance.'

Femi gave a small leap. 'I thought of something! They call her Badger One sometimes.'

Something shifted in Minnie's brain. Something badgery. She handed over the T-shirt slowly. The label caught her eye. Swift Limited. Badgers. Swift ...

'Police Commissioner Swift!' Minnie yelled.

Marcus gave a low moan. Andrew gave him a prod with the tip of the sword.

'We need to call Jimmy right now!' Minnie said.

Chapter Forty-One

'I'm not who you think I am,' Sylvie said firmly.

The car swerved for a second before Anthea got control of it again. 'What? Of course you are. Your name was sewn inside the bridesmaid's dress. I googled you. You were in a play with Betty Massino. I saw your photograph. You're exactly who I think you are.'

'Who do you think she is?' Auntie asked.

'Sylvie Hampshire.'

Auntie raised an eyebrow quizzically at Sylvie.

'No. Well, yes, but no,' Sylvie said.

'What?'

'I *am* Sylvie Hampshire. But it isn't Sylvie Hampshire you're looking for. Flora took the stupid dress to the stupid shop. It was nothing to do with me. Flora is my sister. My twin sister. She took your stupid T-shirt. I don't know anything about it.'

'Twin? Don't be ridiculous.' There was a panicked edge to Anthea's voice. 'You're just trying to wriggle out of this.'

'She is not the one who has made a mistake!' Auntie said forcefully.

'You're *both* trying to wriggle out of this!' Anthea insisted.

Sylvie undid the clasps of her vanity case. She lifted the lid. The rubber smell of her plimsolls wafted upwards. 'I'm going to show you something,' she said. 'If you tell anyone about this, I will be forced to take immediate and desperate action.' Sylvie reached into the case and pulled out her purse. It was a neat little thing. Dad had brought it home from Japan as a present. It had a bright pink flap that folded out like a book cover. Inside the flap was a place for a photograph.

Dad had put a photo there. It showed him and Mum before they split up, with their two twin toddlers – Sylvie and Flora – dressed like something from a Victorian nursery. It was horribly embarrassing, but Sylvie hadn't thrown it out for some reason.

She leaned forwards and waved the purse under Anthea's nose. 'Me. My twin sister,' she said.

'Twins?' Anthea was obviously dazed. The car lurched left before she got it back under control. 'Twins?' Then a slow feline smile spread across her face. 'Well, that changes things. To be honest, I was going to threaten Mrs Adesina here with deportation. But I wasn't completely convinced that the threat would be enough to persuade you – or, rather, your sister – to hand over the T-shirt. After all, Mrs Adesina isn't *her* granny. But to save you? To save her sister? Her twin sister? Well, that's a different kettle of fish, isn't it? I'd say that was much better bait. Sit tight. I think you're staying with me for a while.'

Sylvie looked at Auntie. Fear and panic flashed between them.

What would the police commissioner do now?

They were moving through traffic. Cars and buses and cycles ran parallel with them, but Sylvie knew the drivers couldn't see past the tinted windows, couldn't hear if they shouted, couldn't help them now.

Then the car turned, just beyond the hospital, into a rough, overgrown bit of ground that sometimes served as a car park on very busy days. There was no one there now.

No one except for one white van, parked at the far end of the open ground.

The car drove over gravel. The stones crunched beneath the tyres and the car slowed right down.

The van was parked beside some scrubby bushes.

A tall man got out of the driver's seat. Anthea pulled her car alongside and killed the engine. She got out and pulled open the back door.

'Get out,' she said. 'You're going with Omar.'

Sylvie unclipped her seat belt, grabbed her things and got shakily to her feet. She could feel her heart pumping, her blood racing. She tried to take deep breaths, the way actors with stage fright did. If she didn't calm down, she would burn too much energy. It felt like a long time since she'd eaten that Mars bar.

The deep breaths didn't work.

Omar opened the back door of the van. The inside had metal sides and a wooden floor. A couple of grey woollen blankets had been hastily thrown down. 'Get in,' he said.

'You can't do this! It isn't right!' Sylvie said.

'*Get. In,*' Omar said quietly.

Sylvie got in. Auntie scrambled up behind. It was uncomfortable, cold and smelly, but more than anything else it was terrifying, as Omar closed the door on them and plunged them into darkness.

Chapter Forty-Two

Minnie called Jimmy. He sounded pleased to hear from her, and then she told him that they were on the industrial estate, with Marcus wrapped in packing tape and Sylvie and Gran missing.

'What?' he said. 'What have you been doing? I told you I was investigating.'

'I know,' Minnie said, 'but we couldn't wait. Please, don't be angry, just help us find Gran and Sylvie.'

'Have you any idea where they might be?'

'We think the police commissioner is involved,' Minnie said.

'What?' Jimmy said again. He sounded as though the air was gone from his lungs. '*What?* I don't ... *What?* Listen. I'll be there in ten minutes. You can explain everything to me then. And you'd better have some good evidence this time.'

He hung up.

The others had overheard most of the conversation.

'Do you think we're in trouble?' Andrew said.

'Yes. But as long as Sylvie and Minnie's gran are OK,' Piotr said, 'that's all that matters.'

There was nothing left to do but wait for Jimmy.

Then they heard a phone ring.

It came from Marcus's pocket. His hands were taped behind his back.

'You get it,' Minnie said to Piotr.

Reluctantly, Piotr reached into Marcus's jacket and pulled out the phone. He looked at it and handed it to Minnie.

The caller ID said 'Anthea Swift'.

'Should I answer it?' Minnie asked.

'She's got Sylvie,' Flora said. 'You have to answer it.'

Minnie held the phone to her ear. 'Hello,' she said warily.

'Who's that?' said the voice on the end of the line, a voice Minnie recognised.

'This is Minnie Adesina. Where's my gran?'

'Why, hello, Minnie.' Anthea Swift's voice was silky and assured. 'I was expecting Marcus.'

'He's a bit tied up right now.'

'I see. Is he hurt?'

Minnie looked at Marcus, still on the floor, still scowling. 'No, he's not hurt.'

'Good, because I'd hate to see any violence done on *either* side. Do you understand?'

Minnie knew a threat when she heard one. 'I understand.'

'I knew you were a bright girl. Now, here is what is going to happen. You are going to release Marcus. He will bring you, and only you, to a rendezvous point. You will bring with you the green T-shirt that Flora stole. I will take the green T-shirt. Your grandmother and your friend's sister will then be dropped back home entirely unscathed.'

'And if I say no?'

'Then your grandmother and your friend's sister will both wish you had not.'

Minnie could feel her heart playing drums against her chest. Flora was watching her silently. Piotr, Andrew and Femi all looked tense.

Could she make this right?

It was down to her to try.

She had an idea, but it would be a gamble. She took a deep breath.

'I'm not going to untie Marcus,' she said. 'I don't trust him. I don't trust you either. Here's what's actually going to happen. You will drive to the warehouse on the industrial estate. You will bring Gran and Sylvie with you. I want to know that you haven't hurt a single hair on their heads. Then, and only then, will you get the T-shirt back.'

There was a long pause. Would she agree?

Then Anthea spoke. 'I will be at the warehouse in seven minutes' time. I want you to stand outside, alone, with the T-shirt ready. Anything else and I will reverse right out of there with the hostages. Is that clear?'

'It's clear.'

The line went dead.

Minnie's arm fell to her side, the phone cradled loosely in her fingers. 'Anthea Swift is on her way.'

'We heard,' Flora said. 'She wants you alone. Jimmy won't agree to that.'

Jimmy.

Minnie had forgotten that Jimmy was on his way. Would he come in and take over? Would he spook Anthea and make her drive off with Gran and Sylvie like she'd threatened?

Was there any way he would let her stand alone and hand over evidence? He had to, otherwise it would be Gran and Sylvie who would pay the price.

She heard the sound of a police siren approaching.

Chapter Forty-Three

Minnie ran outside, with the others right behind her. Flora checked her watch. 'We've only got six minutes before the police commissioner gets here,' she said.

A police car pulled into the drive and headed towards them. It stopped by the curb, in plain view of the road.

'They can't park there,' Minnie said.

Both front doors opened and Jimmy stepped out; a woman in police uniform got out too.

'Hello,' she called in a sickly sweet voice. 'What have you little ones been up to?'

Minnie looked at Piotr in horror; the woman clearly thought they were still in nursery. Jimmy strode over to them. He was harassed, his forehead creased with worry. 'Right,' he said, 'you had better tell me exactly what's been going on. I want to hear everything.'

'There isn't time. You have to move your car! Hide it,' Minnie begged.

The woman strolled towards them. She had a wide smile. 'So you're the wonder children I've been hearing so much about from Jimmy. I'm his beat partner, Helena. Now you've made Jimmy very worried. What's all this we hear about Sylvie chasing bad guys on her own?'

'Five minutes,' Flora said. Her voice betrayed her panic.

Minnie glared at Helena. 'Will you stop talking! I have something important to say.'

'Hey!' Jimmy said. 'That's rude and uncalled for.'

Minnie forced down a scream of frustration. Why wouldn't Jimmy just listen to her? 'Sorry,' she managed to say. 'But you don't understand. We need you to hide your car, then hide yourselves and record everything that happens here in the next ten minutes. If you do, you will have all the good solid evidence you need.'

'Evidence for what?' Helena said.

'Evidence to prove that Police Commissioner Anthea Swift is in charge of an international art smuggling gang that uses little kids to carry messages, and kidnaps grandmothers to get their way.'

Jimmy and Helena looked stunned. They froze, their mouths open, as though time had suddenly stopped.

'Four minutes,' Flora said.

Minnie looked Jimmy right in the eye. She tried to look as determined and honest as she possibly could. 'Please, Jimmy, please, you have to trust me.'

Jimmy closed his mouth. He gave a swift nod. 'Helena, move the car.'

'But they can't be right,' Helena said. 'They can't be.'

'Move the car. Take it behind the next building and park out of sight. Then run back here. Run, OK?'

Helena sighed, but ran back to the car and got in.

'Minnie, are you sure about all this?' Jimmy asked.

'You'll see yourself,' Minnie said. 'She's on her way here to take the evidence.'

'Well,' Jimmy said. 'In that case, we'd better be ready.'

Chapter Forty-Four

'Two minutes,' Flora said, checking her watch.

The car was hidden, but the crowd outside the warehouse was too big.

'Flora, Andrew, you need to take Femi inside and keep him safe,' Minnie said.

Femi was still holding his green T-shirt, cradling it like it was his lost teddy bear.

'Femi, please can I take your T-shirt back, just for a bit?' Minnie asked.

Femi frowned, but held it out with both hands. The payment label was creased and crinkled from Femi's hug, but it was still cast-iron evidence against Anthea Swift and she was coming to get it. Flora took Femi's hand and led him inside with Andrew.

Minnie turned to the others. 'Piotr, Jimmy, can you stay out of sight?'

'I want to be close enough to help should you need it.'

'Fine,' Minnie agreed, 'but out of sight.'

'Done. I'll be on foot, at the side of the building. Piotr and Helena, you wait across the road. Everyone else, inside. Stay out of harm's way. For once.'

Dusk was falling properly now and the low sun cast long shadows around the estate: black rectangles, like toppled gravestones. The air was colder. Night was coming.

They all split up. Jimmy slipped behind the end wall of the Swift warehouse and crouched low. Piotr and Helena ran across the street and ducked into the front porch of the unit opposite.

Minnie stood alone on the pavement, watching the drive. It was a black river leading Anthea to them. She cradled the fabric in her arms and waited.

It wasn't long before she heard the sound of an engine approaching. It got louder, then she saw its headlights.

Omar's white van.

It trundled on to the drive. The lights blinded Minnie for a second, then they swung past. She blinked.

She heard the doors click open, then heeled shoes tapping across concrete. Anthea Swift stood before her.

The woman still looked smart – her well-cut suit fitted her perfectly – but a few stray strands of hair were falling from her clasp and her mascara was smudged. There were signs that today wasn't going the way it was meant to.

'Minnie,' Anthea said. 'I'm glad to see you decided to be sensible. Give me the T-shirt.'

'Not until I've seen my gran and Sylvie. I want to know they're safe.'

'They're fine.'

Minnie's hand tightened on the fabric. She stepped backwards. 'No Gran, no T-shirt,' she said.

'Fine,' Anthea said impatiently. 'Omar! Get them out.'

The passenger door opened. Omar paced around the van. Minnie heard the clunk of metal as a lock was opened. Then she saw two shapes stagger to the ground.

'Gran!' she cried. 'Sylvie!'

'Minnie? What are you doing here?' Gran's voice called out. Minnie saw her step forward.

But Omar held out both arms – he stopped Gran and Sylvie in their tracks.

'Now,' Anthea said, 'as you can see, they are well and unharmed. For now. I suggest you give me the T-shirt and they will stay that way.'

Minnie planted her legs apart and folded her arms around the cloth. 'It's Femi's T-shirt, not yours.'

'Femi is not your concern.'

'Is he yours? Was it you who took him away from his family? Or did the Lagos side of operations do that?'

Anthea pressed her lips closed. It was clear she was getting irritated. But it was important to keep her talking.

'Was it you who suggested digging up the heads in the royal burial site? Or did the people in Lagos come up with it? Do you know the king had nightmares?'

'It was a business opportunity, what are a few bad dreams?' Anthea snapped. 'If you are sensible you will conclude this in a businesslike way. The evidence in exchange for your gran. A fair swap. Once it's done, we can all go back to our lives as if this never happened. When I have the T-shirt, we will be filling this van with everything from the storage room,' Anthea said. She rested a pale hand on the side of the van. 'There won't be a single piece of evidence that we were ever here. There will be no point in your going to the police once we've finished.'

Minnie nodded. No point at all. 'I won't go to the police after we're done. I know when I'm beaten. I just want to know, was it you who gave the king nightmares? Or was it Marcus's idea?'

Anthea gave a mirthless laugh. 'Marcus? That lily-livered fool? He wouldn't have the gumption to do any of this if I weren't watching his back every step of the way. Of course it was my idea. Do you really think Omar and Marcus have the contacts, the power, the vision to do it alone? Now, the T-shirt.'

Minnie folded the T-shirt carefully, smoothing down the stained material. She stepped forwards and held it out.

Anthea moved closer, her hands extended.

Minnie jerked the T-shirt out of her reach.

'Minnie,' Anthea said, 'please don't play games with me. You will regret it.'

'Anthea,' Minnie replied. 'You talk too much.'

She tucked the T-shirt under her arm and pulled her mobile phone from her pocket. The red light of the recording app glowed like a beacon in the gloom.

'Jimmy!' Minnie yelled. 'We got everything!'

She heard footsteps running towards them – Jimmy, Helena and Piotr.

Anthea gave a scream of rage and lunged for the phone. Omar grabbed Sylvie and tried to run. She screamed and bit and struggled and swiped at him. Gran laid into him hard with her well-stuffed handbag. He couldn't get more than three steps before Helena threw him against the side of the van and pinned his arms behind his back.

Anthea's hand gripped Minnie's wrist tightly, the two struggled together. Then, Jimmy whipped the phone out from between them.

'I'm sorry, ma'am,' he said, 'but this phone needs to be taken into police evidence. I'm also sorry to tell you that you're under arrest. You have the right to remain silent, you have the right to a solicitor –'

'Don't you dare read me my rights!' Anthea yelled.

Jimmy put a heavy hand on Anthea's shoulder and guided her to stand beside Omar. The sound of wailing police cars drifted towards them through the night air.

The next thing Minnie knew was that Gran had enveloped her in the strongest, longest hug the world had ever known. She was squeezed like the last bit of toothpaste. Gran was half-laughing, half-crying.

'It's OK, Gran, it's OK.' Minnie's words were muffled by Gran's heaving shoulders.

'It is not OK.' Gran finally released her hug, but still held Minnie's arms tightly. 'What terrible things are happening! Why are you here with these awful people and not studying with Sylvie? You know, she has been so brave tonight.' Minnie groaned inwardly; it seemed spending time with Sylvie had made Gran like her more, not less. 'Oh, look, the terrible people are under arrest, at last.'

The squad cars had circled the van and more officers were depositing Anthea and Omar into the backseats. Marcus was escorted out of the unit, flanked by two policemen.

Gran pulled Minnie back into a hug. 'Sylvie has been brave, and you have been brave, and Piotr and Andrew and Flora. My beautiful, brave granddaughter.'

Minnie wrapped her arms tight around Gran.

'The best thing is,' Minnie said, 'I've found your hibiscus tea.'

Chapter Forty-Five

'Turn it left. No, other left. That's it. To you. Wait!' Dad held one end of the bed frame, while Mum's assistant, Bernice, tried to persuade the other end that it wanted to fit through the doorway. Minnie didn't think there was any chance it was going to go, and then, seconds later, Dad found the right angle and the bed was in the corridor. Bernice had said it would be perfect for her son, who was too big for his cot.

The empty space in Minnie's room looked weird. There were dimples in the carpet where the bed legs had been. Suddenly it seemed that her floor was big enough to play football on. She could even open her wardrobe door if she wanted to.

Gran was leaving.

There was the sound of a commotion in the hallway.

More people, hurried greetings, the thump of Bernice dropping her end of the bed.

Minnie stuck her head out of her room to see what was going on.

Jimmy was in the corridor, trying to help carry the bed and climb over it at the same time. It looked as though he were trying to skip with sticks.

Gran had heard him too. She came out of the living room. 'Jimmy!' she said warmly. 'You've come to take me away?'

He took off his hat. 'Good morning, Mrs Adesina, I certainly have.'

Now that it was actually time, Minnie felt hollow, her chest empty as a drum. She dashed across the hall and launched herself at Gran, squeezing her as tight as she could. The scent of spice and flowers, the rough scratch of Gran's cotton dress against Minnie's cheek, felt like home.

'Oh!' Gran gasped. 'It's all right. You will see me every day, won't she, Jimmy?'

Jimmy had hurdled the bed – Minnie could hear Dad and Bernice squabbling as they tried to get it down the stairs. 'Yes, of course you'll see your gran,' he said. 'The flats are right beside the police station, on the way to your school. You can pop in every day.'

'You can do your homework at my kitchen table!' Gran said, patting her shoulder.

Minnie let go of Gran. It was nice she was still going to be in the country, but sad that she wouldn't be sharing a room any more. Jimmy had helped find her a place of her own, with lots of other older people nearby and a matron on call if she needed help. Minnie knew it was for the best, but it still made her feel wobbly.

'A cup of tea before we go,' Gran said.

In the kitchen, Mum was packing up a cardboard box of food to help Gran settle in. Gran lifted her tea from the top of the box and put the kettle on. Jimmy sat at the table. Minnie put herself in charge of finding biscuits.

'So, Jimmy,' Gran said, 'tell us everything. What's been going on with the case?'

It had been nearly a week since the night at the warehouse. Minnie knew that Anthea, Marcus and Omar had been arrested, but it had been a few days since they'd heard any more.

Jimmy took his tea from Gran with a nod. He blew on it thoughtfully before saying, 'We've found Femi's family. His

242

aunt. She owns a farm. He's going to go and live with her. There's no sign of his mum and dad sadly. Which is maybe why he fell into the clutches of the gang in the first place.'

'He's not in any trouble now?' Minnie asked.

'No. He's too young to face any charges. He was being used as a courier, money, communications, all hidden in his luggage. But it's over. Don't worry, he's safe now.'

'And the head?'

'You were right. It had been excavated illegally. The police in Nigeria have traced the thieves. It seems they were behind a few art thefts in the country. Anthea Swift used her connections to smuggle the bronze head out and Marcus was going to sell it on in Europe.' Jimmy took a sip of his drink, then pulled a face. Minnie didn't blame him. Tea shouldn't taste of flowers.

Gran sat down at the table. 'The kings can rest again,' she said.

Jimmy nodded. 'The head will be returned to Nigeria as soon as the investigation is concluded.' He put down his cup. It was still nearly full. 'Well, that was delicious, but I think we'd best be getting on. Shall I take your luggage down to the car?'

'You can take this box,' Mum said, handing him the food. 'We'll be down in a minute with the rest.'

There was a general bustle as Gran rinsed the cups and Jimmy got to his feet. He headed out with the food. Then Dad was back. He took Gran's big red suitcases.

Minnie carried the small black one downstairs. It was only a little thing – light too. But it had started such a big adventure. It just went to show, the small things were important too.

Jimmy's squad car was parked outside the salon. It was allowed in the pedestrian zone. Above, the sky was the bright blue of the sea. An aeroplane had left cotton bud trails. Minnie placed the black case carefully in the boot of the car.

She paused, looking at it. It had led her to Femi, to the head of a king, to an international smuggling ring. It was amazing.

'Mind out,' Dad said. He swung the big red cases up, and the black case was hidden.

Jimmy held open the door for Gran to get in. 'Will you say your goodbyes now?' he asked.

Mum shook her head. 'Don't be silly. We're all coming with you.'

Then Minnie found herself squished in the back of the car, with Mum and Dad on either side and Gran in

Acknowledgements

Thank you to the wonderful Lucy Coats, whose postcard at Folly Farm was so inspirational. To Liz Kessler, who helped to make sure we were all in the same room at the same time. Thanks also to Christian and Ekwy, who read an early draft of this book, checking for cultural errors. Any that still remain are entirely my fault. Thanks to Ellen, Polly, Helen, Jodie, Jane and Julian for their careful steering through an eventful time. And massive thanks to my family for their support; especially Simon, who suggests parallel universes where much worse things happen in order to keep me cheery.

the front. Jimmy turned on the radio. It crackled with police messages, then he pressed a button and music filled the car. He turned up the volume.

Minnie settled back into her seat and smiled.

She hoped the wind changed and they could stay like this forever.